TO BARGAIN WITH A HIGHLAND BUCCANEER

Heart of a Scot
Book Eight

By
COLLETTE CAMERON®

Blue Rose Romance®

Sweet - to - Spicy Timeless Romance®

USA Today Bestselling Author
COLLETTE CAMERON
Sweet-to-Spicy Timeless Romance®

For permission requests, write to the publisher at the address below.
Attn: Permissions Coordinator
info@collettecameronbooks.com
collettecameronbooks.com
eBook ISBN: 978-1-954307-82-7
Print Book ISBN: 978-1-966087-42-7

FREE BOOK!

JOIN MY EXCLUSIVE MAILING LIST
Collette Cameron Newsletter

AND GET A FREE EBOOK!

https://collettecameronbooks.com/freegift

Plus Sneak Peeks, Giveaways, Contests, Exclusive Content, and More... P.S. I promise only good stuff ~ **no** spam!

DEDICATION

For every reader who adores Highlanders, pirates, swashbucklers, and buccaneers.

ONE

12 April 1721
Holyrood Abbey
Leith, Scotland

Branwen Glanville couldn't prevent the slight shiver parading the length of her spine as she craned her neck, studying what was left of Holyrood Abbey's majestic chapel. Though sunny —the sky was a bright blue—the crisp air held an unmistakable chill.

Not at all uncommon for coastal Scotland—any part of Scotland, for that matter.

And yet, as accustomed as she was to Scotland's less than genial clime, another shudder rippled through her. Almost— *aye, almost*—as if in premonition of something sinister or ominous.

But what?

Holding her hood in place against the persistent, briny breeze tugging at the soft material, she glanced around the sun-drenched grounds. The golden rays shining through the remnants of the church's elaborate entrance cast striking shadows on the lush green lawns spread out below.

Nothing struck her as odd or drew her attention despite the overall atmosphere of melancholy and decades of awed reverence permeating the holy remains.

So why couldn't she shake this unwarranted sense of unease?

A dozen or so other people besides her family wandered the ruins as the mischievous breeze toyed with the long blades of verdant grass, plump, newly budded leaves, and the hem of her cloak with impartial precociousness.

Drawing her dark plum-colored velvet cloak tighter, she squinted at a rook watching her from atop an elaborately constructed arched stone wall. The light glinted off the bird's glossy plumage—an almost metallic blue hue colored its black wings. It dipped its head, rubbing its beak several times against the pale stone before flying off amid raucous squawks.

Probably to join its family or mayhap feed its young. In the distance, she watched as four other rooks joined the first. As they arched and spiraled their way through the sky, another three flew in loudly to meet them.

Unlike many people, she didn't believe crows, ravens, or rooks portended evil. In fact, she admired the species for their intelligence, cleverness, and dedication to their families.

Mayhap she was partial to them because her name meant blessed or fair raven, depending on which Welsh translation one preferred.

She squinted at the birds as they became smaller and smaller, eventually fading from sight in the distance. Although, now that she pondered on it, a gathering of crows *was* called a murder and a group of ravens a conspiracy.

Crows and ravens arena rooks, she chided herself.

Nae, but they are related.

Shaking her head once to dismiss her silly ruminations, Branwen returned her regard to the once glorious hallowed building.

Farther along the impressive bones of the abbey, Branwen's guardian, Keane Buchannan, the Duke of Roxdale, held his stepdaughter Cora's hand and his wife, Marjorie, held her other daughter Elana's hand as they inspected a pair of empty stone coffins.

Many decades before—perhaps centuries even—nameless marauders had desecrated the graves, possibly in search of a valuable bauble or two. Or perchance, the vaults had been plundered during the Reformation when one religious order believed itself superior to another.

That ideology hadn't changed much in the centuries since, truth be told.

It mattered naught why the burial places had been ransacked, but Branwen felt a peculiar sense of pity for the dead who hadn't been permitted a peaceful eternal slumber. Even as fascinated as she was with history, it didn't seem right to disturb the deceased simply out of curiosity.

Och, well.

She gave a little roll of her shoulder.

What was done was done.

She trailed her gaze over the well-maintained grounds once more. Though only a mere shadow of its former splendor, the abbey possessed an eerie beauty as well as an aura of sadness. The passage of time had been much kinder to the adjacent palace.

Giving herself another mental shake for her morose musings on such a lovely day, Branwen raised her face to the sun. Allowing her eyelids to lower, she inhaled the refreshing air. It held the tang of the sea but also the pungent scent of freshly cut grass and the faintest fragrance of fruit tree blossoms wafting from the palace gardens.

Though Edinburgh was scarcely two miles away, Leith's air was far cleaner. No dingy, soot-laden clouds lingered overhead, blanketing all and sundry in choking gray, in large part due to the persistent winds blowing inland from the Firth of Forth.

Girlish giggles carried to her on that same insistent wind, and she opened her eyes, sweeping her mouth upward.

Elana and Cora were thoroughly enjoying today's outing. Grinning, exposing the front tooth she'd lost but two days ago, Cora waved at Branwen as she skipped beside her new papa, pointing at one thing or another.

Keane nodded with an appropriate amount of interest and genuine affection.

Branwen waved back, smiling in return.

She adored Marjorie's daughters, and Marjorie too. She was the older sister that Branwen and her sister, Bethea, had never had. Sweet-tempered, patient, but with a will of iron, she'd made a brilliant duchess. But more importantly, she'd taken to Keane's wards with genuine caring and friendship.

Branwen and her sister adored her.

At the thought of Bethea, Branwen's chest tightened, and her breath caught as if someone had pulled her stays far too tight. Loneliness and no small amount of worry vied for supremacy in the tangled knots where her stomach ought to be.

At this very moment, her dear sister and her new husband, Camden Kennedy, were cloistered at Glen Tormallan Lodge —Keane's hunting lodge outside Culloden—hiding from spies that had meant them harm.

All because in March, Branwen had injured her feet during an unfortunate dance with a cloddish lord, and Bethea had tried to help her. Branwen had craved the excitement of Edinburgh's social life until that fateful night when her sister had been abducted after overhearing a plot to depose the king.

Thankfully, the spies had been apprehended, and Bethea and Camden were safe.

Now, however, Branwen found she far preferred the many historical sites in and around Edinburgh, as well as Leith's fascinating seaport, to social gatherings. And she missed the Highland's craggy beauty more than she'd imagined possible.

Stepping over a rock, which likely had fallen from the abbey's missing ceiling, Branwen mused to herself. She supposed as the daughter of a ship's captain, perhaps a bit of mariner's blood ran in her veins.

Until recently, she'd not thought a great deal about her father's livelihood. After all, she'd been a wee lass of five when her parents had been lost at sea during a tempest.

Raised at Trentwick Castle, high in the Scottish Highlands, she'd never realized how much the ocean appealed to her. But the sound of the waves greeting the shore, the briskness of the playful breeze, and the strident calls of the sea birds touched something deep within her.

Stirred something. Awoken a hunger Branwen hadn't known she possessed.

With a final glance at the abbey, she retraced her steps to the entrance and gazed in the direction of Leith's docks. As much as she'd enjoyed poking around the church's ruins, her real interest lay at the port, where the masts of ship after ship stood in the distance like faithful, nautical sentinels.

A yearning to board one of those vessels and sail into the sunset, headed for foreign lands, engulfed her. At the inexplicable longing, her breath and heart stalled for a heartbeat.

Such a wish was a fanciful dream. Keane held no interest

in ever leaving Scotland. Marjorie either, for that matter. She even abhorred travel by coach.

A small frown puckered Branwen's brow.

Her guardian and his wife were as content to remain in Scotland their entire lives as mice in a well-stocked larder.

Pursing her mouth, she hunched further into her heavy cloak, wishing she'd worn a heavier woolen gown and shawl.

She hadn't considered that after walking here, spending an hour or so poking around the ruins, and then walking into Leith before returning to Edinburgh, she might become chilled. That had been foolish of her, but she wasn't about to complain or express her discomfort.

Keane had agreed—after considerable cajoling—that they might stroll the docks and admire the many ships in port, accompanied by Keane's friend, Bryston McPherson. Bryston had recently returned from his mission in England. In point of fact, he'd been appointed to deliver one of the traitors responsible for Bethea's abduction to His Majesty's dungeons.

He was to meet them at eleven of the clock, the only reason Keane had agreed to Branwen's request to explore the abbey and wharf.

A seafaring man himself but also an agent for the crown, at six feet, four inches tall and comparable in size to an oak tree, Bryston would act as their unofficial bodyguard and tour guide.

Oh, Branwen wasn't fooled as to why Keane had asked Bryston to accompany them.

Scarred and tattooed, his Viking heritage on display for all to see, the Highland warrior fairly exuded power, strength, and intimidation. In truth, he'd frightened the stuffing out of her the first time she'd come upon him in the great hall eight years ago—before he'd acquired the scar that ran the length of his cheek now.

She'd been a gangly twelve-year-old in braids, and he a strapping nineteen-year-old, wilder than even the untamed Scots she'd become accustomed to. Then he'd winked and given her a crooked smile—an almost boyish grin—and her fear had dissipated as swiftly as fog upon a loch in the summer sun.

Bryston possessed stormy eyes—deterrents to unwanted conversation—a marble-like jaw, a mouth generally pulled into an unyielding, grim line, and a warrior's sculpted form, which made men and women tremble.

The former in fear and the latter in feminine awareness.

Not that she suffered from such womanly afflictions.

Good heavens, nae.

Truth be known, men of his ilk paraded in and out of Trentwick regularly. She was hardly the sort of woman to turn into a quivering custard at the site of a virile man's flexing muscles or a beard-stubbled jawline.

However, with Bryston and Keane in attendance as they visited the wharf, no one with a lick of common sense would cast so much as a gimlet eye in Branwen and Marjorie's direction today.

Naturally, even accompanied by two capable protectors, neither she nor Marjorie would be permitted to wander the unsavory lanes that always seemed to stretch out from dockyards like great depraved vines.

Still, Bryston had advised Keane that there was a charming tavern on Abbey Strand, which provided a partial view of the harbor, where they might partake in a midday meal before returning to Edinburgh this afternoon.

Branwen sighed as she reached the abbey's arched entrance and rested a shoulder against the nearly five-centuries-old structure. She wasn't sure what had plagued her of late, but a discontentment whirled through her at least once a day.

In general, it occurred when she permitted her mind to wander to her future and contemplated what her life would be like now that Bethea was married. Keane too. She felt as if she were an unnecessary fifth wheel. No one would ever hint at any such thing, but what newlyweds wanted another person underfoot constantly?

Only, she wasn't sure what it was she wanted. What, precisely, it was that she lacked or craved. Or why this new unrest seemed to expand daily. At Trentwick Castle, she'd believed it was because Keane had been so protective, rarely allowing her or Bethea to attend any functions.

He'd had his reasons, of course.

Good reasons, in truth.

His own mother had been set upon, ravished, and impregnated by a blackguard. Marjorie—bless the woman—had been instrumental in convincing him to relax his strictures and permit his wards this time in Edinburgh.

Undeniably, Branwen had enjoyed the balls, assemblies, and routs. Though, in all honesty, she'd found Edinburgh's High Society somewhat less than cordial. Downright feral at times, if she were perfectly candid.

As she scanned the horizon, a tall, solidly built man caught her attention, and a queer fluttering began behind her breast-bone as if a half dozen blue tits were trapped there before throttling to her throat.

Bryston McPherson.

TWO

The Scot truly was a most pleasant visual feast for Branwen's appreciative feminine regard.

As was his wont, Bryston wore his pale blond hair braided and pulled back at the sides. He left the rest of the fair strands trailing past his shoulders. The slight breeze flirted with the tendrils, lifting them playfully before dropping them onto the vast expanse of his black-clad back and shoulders where they contrasted starkly.

Lord, but the man possessed a splendid physique.

More than once, Branwen had seen him without his shirt as he practiced his warrior's skills in the bailey with Keane and the other clansmen. Unlike many of the Scots who sported thick patches of hair upon their chests, only a light smattering of blond hair graced the cleft between his ridiculously large, bronzed pectoral muscles.

A tattoo of a dolphin and a red rose extended from his right shoulder and around his bicep.

Of a sudden, Branwen grew inexplicably heated, warmth washing over her in a powerful wave of awareness.

She veered her attention lower, lest Bryston catch her openly admiring him.

Admirin'?

Ye were oglin' the mon, plain and simple.

And did her inner diatribe and self-recrimination curb her assessment?

Nae, indeed. Not a jot.

She continued her visual assessment, very much liking what she saw.

Practical boots covered the lower half of his thickly muscled legs clad in black leather. The sleek, sculpted flesh rippled and rolled with his confident stride. As usual, a jewel-handled dagger glinted from the belt at his trim waist, and a sword swung near his lean hips.

Unlike other Scots, he seldom wore plaid, even as a waist-coat. He preferred the long, black leather doublet he wore today. Only the snow-white shirt and luxurious maroon scarf tied at the column of his corded, sun-browned throat inter-rupted the monotony of his ensemble.

The sunlight caught the long sliver of scar that lashed across his left cheek, but rather than disfiguring his face, she'd long ago decided the mark rather gave him a dashing pirate effect. He even sported a ruby earring in his left ear, although his wasn't a large, gaudy looped affair, but instead, a half-circle studded with blood-red gems.

A tempting pirate, indeed.

And was it any wonder?

The man *had* been a buccaneer—a privateer—for His Majesty for several years. Once, when she'd been fourteen, she'd accidentally overheard that tidbit. Branwen had also learned Bryston had gone to sea at the tender age of ten and owned his own ship by one and twenty.

No small feat, that.

However, no one ever discussed Bryston McPherson's life as a swashbuckler openly. Nor the reason he'd abruptly given up his wandering the oceans several years ago.

Two burly men flanked him, the threesome advancing toward the abbey with measured gaits.

Assessing them, she cocked her head.

Most definitely *not* Scots.

One possessed skin the color of smooth, dark honey, and the other almond-shaped eyes and an extravagant mustache. They sported two dirks apiece in their waistbands, as well as swords. Were they sailors or men Bryston had brought along as bodyguards?

Surely, the wharf wasn't so very dangerous as all of that. Why, even urchins scampered about the piers alone delivering messages and running errands.

Perchance the extra security had something to do with Bethea's abduction and the despicable Earl of Montieth who was behind the act.

Nae, that couldn't be the reason. The strapping man advancing toward her had seen Montieth arrested for treason. The earl might very well have met a gruesome end by now.

Finally noticing her, Bryston changed his direction, his sturdy legs and elongated treads carrying him to her in short order. As usual, his guarded eyes hid his thoughts as effectively as shutters secured across windows.

The daunting men followed him, their alert gazes taking in every inch of the churchyard. Had she come upon them in another setting, they might've frightened her.

Bryston nodded his blond head, those dark coffee-brown eyes of his hooded and reserved and so unexpected given his champagne-colored hair. "Miss Glanville."

Hmm, she'd been Branwen for years.

Why the formality now?

She slid a surreptitious glance at the other men.

Because of his companions?

Bryston possessed a deliciously deep voice, but rather than rough or grating, his speech flowed forth with a lyrical quality. Possibly because he possessed an extraordinary talent for singing, mostly naughty ditties or soulful seamen's ballads.

"*Mr.* McPherson." Arching an eyebrow, she righted herself and returned his formal greeting before offering a sincere smile to the men accompanying him.

They gave brief, polite nods but remained silent and *alert?*

One of Bryston's eyebrows shied upward at her coolly polite tone as if he knew precisely what she was thinking.

"Roxdale?" As always, Bryston was a man of few words.

"Keane and the others are just there." She turned to point them out but instead pulled the corners of her brows together.

Where had they gone to?

He followed her stare and braced one broad hand on his hip, a sudden tautness settling over him. Tattoos adorned several of his fingers, and a plain gold band encircled his little finger.

Eyes narrowed and legs splayed, his companions fingered their swords.

Unease fairly oozed from the trio.

What in the world?

"Where?" Bryston asked succinctly, scraping his astute gaze over the abbey and the other sightseers.

"They were near that pair of coffins." Wrinkling her nose, Branwen tucked a stray strand of black hair behind her ear that was tickling her cheek. "I suppose they might've gone around to the other side. There's a graveyard there. It's quite fascinating. Some of the stones date back several centuries."

He angled his head, sliding his attention in the direction she'd indicated. "Zhao, ye and Bayu find Roxdale and his family and escort them to the Queen's Arms. Use caution and apprise the duke of the situation. I'll go ahead of ye with Miss Glanville."

According to Keane, the tavern and eatery they were to have their midday meal at was a scant half-mile away.

Wait. Situation?

What situation?

"Come along, Miss Glanville," Bryston said without preamble, taking her elbow. All the while that keen gaze of his roved the landscape.

What did he seek? Or who?

"Why?" she asked with a touch of starch in her tone.

"Plans have changed," he said curtly.

She dug her heels into the soft grass.

"Pray, explain yerself." Casting a glance over her shoulder, she caught sight of his men disappearing around the priory's other open end.

"I canna assist Keane today." He glanced down at her, the corners of his eyes tight and the irises so small that she felt as if she gazed into warm chocolate pools. Light blond bristle covered his jaw, and a muscle flexed there on the right side. "I must be away as soon as I ken ye and the others are safe."

A steely inflection in his tone caused her heart to leap and flutter against her ribs.

"Why, Bryston? What has happened?"

At his urging, she fell into pace beside him.

"An old enemy was sighted in Leith nae more than an hour ago."

"*Enemy?*" Her mouth had gone dry as cold ash, and she licked her lower lip. "Does this have somethin' to do with yer days as a buccaneer?"

He gave a sharp nod and propelled her forward. "We have

nae time to waste, lass. I must see ye safe before I sail with the tide."

"Yer leavin'?" She tried to sort her jumbled thoughts, not at all certain why that knowledge dismayed her. Perhaps because he'd only returned and he was rather a permanent fixture at Trentwick these past several months? "I thought ye didna sail anymore."

"I still own a ship." He didn't elaborate.

To her knowledge, he hadn't set foot upon in years, and he'd remained remarkably closemouthed as to why.

His pace didn't ease as he ushered her along beside him. Just like a man. Drag her with him because *he* was in danger, but refuse to explain what, exactly, was going on.

"Are those men ye sent after Keane part of yer crew?" They looked like what she'd always envisioned swashbucklers would.

"Aye."

They'd reached the dirt track leading to the main road by then, and she looked behind her once more. There was still no sign of Keane, Marjorie, or the girls.

Mayhap they'd taken a tour of Holyrood Palace, which abutted the abbey. Elana had expressed a wish to do so.

"Why canna I wait for Keane and Marjorie?" Apprehension raised her nap hair as she quickened her pace to keep up with him. It wasn't that she was afraid of Bryston. She wasn't.

In point of fact, she'd sensed something was amiss before he'd arrived.

"Because I dinna ken if I was followed, and I'd see ye tucked away first." His hand flexed around her elbow, and it occurred to her that he deliberately kept her near his side.

Shielding her?

From what?

Another tremor of alarm winged through her, causing her stomach to sink in that weird hollow way it did when she was startled or unnerved.

"And because my enemy was askin' questions about ye and Roxdale that I dinna like," Bryston elucidated.

"Couldna ye have simply sent a note instead?" Branwen knitted her brow. Wasn't he also endangering her and her family by meeting them at the Queen's Arms?

She scooted her focus to the trees and shrubberies, viewing the area with new attentiveness and misgivings as wariness settled upon her.

Was this the reason she'd been unnerved earlier?

Had she sensed something was afoot?

Never as jolly or charming as Camden or Graeme Kennedy, or any of Keane's other friends, the intense, alert man beside her had become a stranger.

"Nae." His jaw spasmed, but he stared straight ahead, his slightly imperfect profile a testament to his nose once having been broken.

"Ye need to trust me, Branwen. I canna take the time to explain right now."

Back to Branwen now, was he?

The bloody man blew hot and cold, as fickle as a female cat in heat.

"This disna make any sense," Branwen said, tugging forcefully to free her arm.

She didn't know Bryston well enough to toddle off with him, much less trust the man.

Well, she *knew* him, of course.

He was a particular friend of her guardian's, after all. She'd even danced with him once at the Hogmanay celebration last year. But she didn't know *this* Bryston McPherson, the buccaneer turned covert agent.

Slightly breathless at their rapid pace, she searched her surroundings again.

The quaint village loomed before them.

Cozy, peaceful, unremarkable.

Cobbled streets and stone structures lined Easter Road, the main entrance. The ships' masts gently rose and fell as the water lapped at the vessels' bellies. Dozens of men and women milled about the busy streets as carts and wagons lumbered back and forth from the docks.

Two men on horseback rode down the center of the lane, and a young boy ran across the street with a big brown dog, barking at his side. A gray and white cat sat contentedly upon a stone step before an establishment, its eyes half-closed.

Nothing appeared the least amiss.

Nonetheless, unease slithered down her spine and coiled in her belly as her conscience hissed a warning in her ears.

"I think ye'd better let me return to my family, Bryston." She despised the slight tremor in her tone.

However, he didn't give any indication he'd heard her.

"Bryston?" she said again, much more forcefully.

"Have yer feet completely healed?" he asked abruptly, cutting her the briefest glance.

What?

What a peculiar thing to ask.

"Aye. My toes were mostly bruised. I've been fine for over a week now."

Bryston made a rough sound in his throat that almost sounded like a curse. He tightened his grip on her arm as he jutted his bold chin and said almost conversationally, "Branwen, see the mast flyin' a flag with a dolphin and red rose?"

A trio of seedy men emerged from a building and stared boldly at her and Bryston. One bore a long russet beard and a flamboyant red hat, complete with swaying crimson and black ostrich feathers. The other pair wore ill-fitting sailor's garb, and even at this distance, she could see their sweat-stained collars, underarms, and overall griminess.

Alarm surged through her, and she tore her attention away.

Squinting at the horizon, she spotted the striking flag Bryston had directed her attention to. It was quite similar to the tattoo adorning his arm.

Nae coincidence, that.

With her attention fixed on the fluttering rectangle, she nodded. "Aye. I see it."

"That's my ship, *The Dolphin,* and our destination. When we get to the next corner, we're goin' to turn right, and ye need to run as fast as ye can," Bryston murmured low and soothingly as if it were the most natural thing in the world to say.

"*What?*" She shot him an astounded look, fear zigzagging an irregular path from her heart to her throat and raising every single pore on her arms and back. "Why?"

Again, he dropped his earnest gaze to hers for a second. Her eyes clashed with his, now darkened to slate. Tension slanted his dark blond brows into a taut line. "We've been spotted."

"Bryston McPherson, I'm nae takin' another step until ye tell me what's goin' on." Once more, she dug her heels in and came to a stop. It would be the height of folly to blithely go off with him without knowing what caused such a reaction from him.

But wasn't that what she'd just done? Left the abbey at his insistence?

Hold yer wheesht, she berated her too-logical conscience.

"Damn it, lass. I dinna have time to explain all to ye now."

Bryston cast a harrowed glance down the road, his expression growing grimmer by the second. The lyrical cadence of his voice became brusque and steely. "Ye *must* trust me, Branwen."

Branwen also looked to where he stared, and a chill raised gooseflesh from her shoulders to waist this time.

The three menacing men advanced in their direction, their movements orchestrated and predatory.

Danger. Danger. Danger.

Her heart pounded a warning cadence.

A sly, evil smile quirked the mouth of the man with the ridiculous hat.

Och, God.

"Bryston. They are the enemy ye spoke of, arena they?"

"Aye," he said, fisting his hand and looking as if he'd seen a ghost.

"Who are they?"

"The men who killed my wife." He slid his hand down her arm to grasp her hand. "Now run!"

THREE

12 April 1721
Leith, Scotland

Bryston seized Branwen's fine-boned hand and hauled the raven-haired, pewter-eyed beauty with him as he sprinted down the crowded track. She was tall for a woman and kept pace with him, her hand clutching his as if her life depended upon it.

It very well might, damn it to hell.

Her breath rasped in and out, but she didn't slow her pace nor complain.

Another time, he'd have admired her bravery and resolve. At present, however, his mind raced ahead of his pounding feet, plotting the best escape route.

How was it a man that Bryston had believed dead for years walked the streets of Leith? A man he despised with such loathing that his blood boiled and fury blurred his vision?

"McPherson!"

He cringed upon hearing that hated singsong voice.

"I see you and your lovely mademoiselle. I wonder, *mon*

amie, will she meet the same fate as the *belle* Delphine, *oui*?" The French pirate, Marc-André Le Sauvage—*not his real surname but one he'd earned because of his brutal acts*—bellowed in his thick French accent, followed by a deranged laugh.

The man *was* a savage in every way.

Aye, and mad too.

"Jesus on the blessed cross," Branwen panted, glancing over her shoulder, her unbound hair a flowing ebony curtain. Her bright cloak billowed around her ankles as they flew down the street dodging people.

"Bryston, who is that man?"

Nae one ye ever want to meet, lass.

"Who is Delphine?" she gasped between breaths and slanted a harried look over her shoulder. "How does he ken ye?"

Her questions would have to wait.

"Out of the way. Move aside," Bryston shouted, stretching his legs into a sprint, only to slow his progress to dash around a startled elderly woman clutching an overflowing basket to her ample, sagging chest.

Dammit.

They'd never outrun Le Sauvage and his henchmen with this many people milling about.

Indignant men and women exclaimed and protested as Bryston rudely shoved them aside without apology. Behind him, the Frenchman shouted his name again before he ordered his men to pursue Bryston and Branwen.

"*Zut.* After them, Bisonette, Faucheux. They must not escape."

Shite.

Bryston turned down another street, this one narrower and less populated but reeking of refuse. A pair of rats scampered into a hole in the foundation. His heart stampeded in his chest, battering his ribs, and his pulse pounded a frenetic staccato in his ears.

The rumors of Le Sauvage's death had been just that. Rumors.

God's teeth.

And in the ensuing almost five years since he'd seen the devil's spawn and learned of his supposed death at sea, Bryston had become complacent.

But, by God, why wouldn't he have?

I believed the bastard dead and burnin' in the ninth layer of hell right next to the devil himself.

The blackguard was supposed to be dead—his ship lost in the Indian Ocean during a gale.

Somehow, the bastard had survived and had come back to haunt Bryston. His gut wrenched as a vision of Delphine's waxen face and glassy eyes staring sightlessly up at him drove a rusty blade deep into his innards.

Not now! Later, when Branwen was safe, he could permit the old feelings and memories to bubble to the surface.

"This way. Hurry!" He towed a winded Branwen onto a cross street.

He raced them down another lane, weighing his options. Had he been by himself, he'd not be as worried, but Branwen drastically complicated a successful escape.

Though she hadn't said a word, she'd begun to tire. She stumbled, gasped, then caught her footing and kept going. She labored for breath. Little wheezing sounds came from her parted mouth and her hand still clutched his in a finger-numbing grip.

The port lay several streets away, and who knew how many of Le Sauvage's other men patrolled them, this very minute, looking for Bryston?

Likely, they watched his ship as well.

The last time he'd seen that French cockscum's reviled face, Bryston had cradled Delphine's lifeless, blood-soaked body in his arms and been only a hair's breadth away from death himself. The scar on his cheek from the wound that had nearly killed him that day pulled tautly as a feral grimace skewed his face, and a primal growl erupted from his throat.

Her features pinched with terror, Branwen cut him a swift, searching look.

"Dinna stop, lass."

He'd vowed to kill that scurvy dog after Le Sauvage had murdered his beloved wife—slashing her golden skin and inflicting burns, time after time, trying to force information from her she had no knowledge of.

Because there wasn't any goddamned bloody treasure— never had been as far as Delphine knew.

Memories tumbled over one another, a riot of unsolicited and unwelcome recollections surging to the forefront of his mind.

How often had Bryston tenderly called Delphine the treasure of his heart? For she had been. A precious, irreplaceable jewel.

Glancing upward, he recognized his location: Lucky Spence's House.

What if...?

Bryston hesitated for half a blink before making an abrupt decision. Wrapping his arm around Branwen's waist, he unceremoniously propelled her into the nearest building.

She yelped in surprise but didn't resist.

After slamming the door hard enough to rattle the frame, he bolted it from inside.

The commotion brought the voluptuous madam stomping into the entry.

"What the hell do ye—?"

Upon spying him, Abbie Maduthy's demeanor completely transformed. Buxom and curvy, the scantily attired redhead smiled seductively and sashayed forward.

Praise the saints.

Abbie still worked here. Bryston's gamble might just pay off.

"Och, well, if it isna Captain McPherson himself," she all but cooed coyly. "'Tis been a long, *long* time." She flicked a swift, inquisitive glance at Branwen. "Lucky isna here, if that's who ye're lookin' for."

Though he'd never sampled her wares, or any of the other lasses working for Lucky Spence, for that matter, Abbie always made the offer. Bryston's relationship with the establishment had been a business arrangement between Lucky Spence and himself. Lucky had offered the services of his lasses, but Bryston had always declined.

The proprietor required fancy French brandy and other hard-to-find items for his house of pleasure, which Bryston frequently came upon when plundering vessels upon the high seas. It had been quite a lucrative arrangement, benefiting both men, since Bryston had no use for the goods that were often his form of payment.

His Majesty was perpetually and invariably short of gold to pay those in his employ.

"Nae, that's no' why I'm here, Abbie," he said, swiftly scrutinizing the whorehouse for danger while straining his ears for the slightest sounds of pursuit.

Two other women, one blonde, the other brunette, sauntered down the stairs at the end of the corridor, each also boldly displaying their wares.

They were new lasses. Or at least new since he'd last been here six years ago.

"Och, take a peek at *him*," the blonde crooned, cradling her bountiful breasts in her hands provocatively. Licking her lips, she nudged her companion. "I bet he'd satisfy us both, Violet. More than once."

"Aye, he's a braw one, he is," the brunette agreed, pulling her dusky rose satin wrapper aside to display a shapely thigh as she boldly stared at his groin.

His manhood didn't so much as twitch with carnal interest.

Whores had never been his preference for intimate encounters.

Branwen inhaled a sharp breath, and after shooting him an accusatory glare with those speaking gray eyes, pointed her attention to the floor. A blush turned the flawless skin of her cheeks bright pink as she, no doubt, accurately deduced just what sort of establishment he'd dragged her into.

An unfamiliar flush heated his neck. Not because of the prostitutes. No sailor worth his salt colored at the mere presence of a harlot. They were as common in ports as the sea salts who vied for their favors.

Nae, it was the way Branwen looked askance at him. And, by God, that rankled. He wasn't accountable to her.

Nevertheless, Roxdale would skewer him for exposing her to such women. Multiple times, and rightly so.

Aye, but at least Bryston would keep the duke's ward alive.

Abbie clapped her hands once, pointing a cosmetic-laden, stern gaze at the two women still loitering in the entry. "Ye have patrons awaitin' ye already. Go on with ye."

She inclined her head toward the room at the end of the corridor.

Pouts on their rouged lips, the pair gave Bryston one final appreciative glance, their interest apparent, before they reluctantly wandered into what he knew to be the drawing room at the end of the hallway where patrons waited. Given the time of day, they were likely men in Leith for the day and looking for a good time before they returned to their wives and farms.

"Yer in a wee bit of a hurry, Captain," Abbie observed, taking Branwen's measure, from her wind-mussed hair, reddened cheeks, and costly cloak to her fine leather shoes. "I see ye brought yer own entertainment. The lasses willna be happy about that."

Branwen sucked in a sharp breath and cast the woman an affronted look. "I'm no'—"

"Aye, we require a room." He tightened his arm about her waist, causing her to release a startled squeak, and winked at Abbie. "And a place to hide, if ye would oblige us."

The brothel-keeper's red-brown eyebrows shied high on her forehead before she nodded slowly, eyeing Branwen again. This time with considerably more interest.

Damnation.

Bryston should've told Branwen to pull her hood up. Hers was an arresting face, and one didn't forget such beauty. Too late now. As a madam of a brothel, Abbie knew how to keep her mouth shut. He'd make it worth her while.

"Aye, I can," Abbie agreed, her blue eyes narrowing calculatingly. "But it will cost ye."

He produced his most charming grin while warning Branwen to stay silent by pressing his palm firmly into her waist.

She speared him a furious look, her lips pressed so tightly together that white lines bracketed her mouth. He didn't fool himself that she'd keep her thoughts to herself. Nae, the instant they were alone, she'd give him a tongue lashing.

"Ye ken, Abbie, I am *verra* generous."

Branwen made a strangled sound, as if she'd swallowed

pickled eggs whole and they'd become stuck in her throat, which caused Abbie to throw back her head and guffaw.

Branwen took the opportunity to stomp on his toes with her heel.

He stifled a grunt and dug his fingertips into her ribs in a silent warning to behave herself.

She ground her heel harder.

Little hellion.

"Aye, that ye are, Captain." Abbie turned toward the stairs, saying over her shoulder, "Do I need to provide a *diversion* too?"

Her gaze slid to Branwen, and she arched a cynical eyebrow.

He knew exactly the type of diversion she referred to, but he was reluctant to expose Branwen to any more than she'd already seen. Unfortunately, if Le Sauvage and his thugs suspected they were here and chose to search the brothel, something scandalous might be necessary to deter him.

Not meeting Branwen's wide eyes, which had taken on the stormy pewter gray of the North Sea in wintertime, he gave a terse nod. "Aye. That would be appreciated."

"I have just the place for ye." Without waiting for them to follow, the bawd started up the stairs, her loosely tied violet robe swirling about her ankles.

"Bryston," Branwen hissed, trying to squirm free of his hold. Ire and chagrin sparked in her quicksilver eyes. "What do ye think yer doin' draggin' me into a... a *house of ill-repute?*"

He took in her pale features and black-lashed eyes that, for all of her bravado, couldn't entirely hide her fear and apprehension.

"Tryin' to save yer life."

"Why is that man after ye?" Her eyes narrowed further, and sparks flew from their depths. "Why did he kill yer wife?"

A lesser man would've been burnt to cinders by the accusation flaming in her gaze.

"And why is it, Bryston, nae one kens ye were married? No' even Keane."

Because Delphine had been a precious flower, and her death eviscerated me. Left me half a man.

Speaking of the woman who'd been his wife for three short months was beyond Bryston. Yes, he'd gone on with his life, but he'd been forever altered. In truth, he didn't much give a damn whether he lived or died.

But now that he knew Le Sauvage lived, he *did* have a purpose. *Revenge.* He'd see that cur dead by his hand if it was the last thing he ever did. For Delphine. She must be avenged, he vowed to himself.

He guided Branwen's stiff body toward the stairs. Reluctance was clear in her every grudging step. "I'll explain all later, lass. But for now, we need to hide."

FOUR

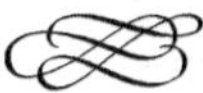

12 April 1721
Lucky Spence's House
Leith, Scotland

If Le Sauvage caught her...

Nae. Nae.

Bryston refused to contemplate the revolting, gut-wrenching notion.

Pressing her full lips into a piqued line, Branwen cast an uneasy glance at the door.

Outside, gruff male voices called to each other, but it was impossible to tell if they belonged to their pursuers.

Nonetheless, it was enough to compel her to agree. Nodding, her wavy ebony hair brushing her shoulders and arms, she hurried up the steps before Bryston.

Bryston raised his eyes ceilingward, releasing a breath and a silent prayer of thanks.

He'd been prepared to toss the obstinate lass over his shoulder if she refused to cooperate. Which meant gagging her and possibly tying her hands and feet too. And if she still didn't quiet, he would have dosed her with the opium he knew full well Abbie kept locked away for special guests.

Bringing his attention back to the woman stamping up the stairs before him, he sighed. As much as he'd loved his wife, there was no denying Branwen Glanville had a delectable form and an angelic face. And, it seemed, she possessed a feisty spirit he hadn't noticed prior to this.

When Bryston found himself observing the tantalizing sway of her hips, despite his avowal not to, he clenched his jaw and pointed his attention upward again.

She's Keane's ward.

He'll have my bollocks and hang them at Trentwick's entry for even thinkin' untoward thoughts about the lass.

Aye, but he'd have to be dead not to notice the alluring woman ascending the risers in front of him. She was the type of woman people stopped and took a second look at.

Her blue-black hair shone like the moon itself. Matching ebony brows arched over clear gray eyes that fluctuated in color from dark pewter to silver. Skin as smooth and creamy as statues he'd seen in Greece covered delicately formed bones, sloping cheeks, a high brow, and a rosebud of a chin.

And her lips.

God's teeth, her plump, ripe lips were full and usually tinted berry-red, enticing men to taste their sweetness.

Aye, Branwen Glanville might be a beauty, but she was not for him. His heart had died the day Delphine had, and he'd buried the shredded organ with his golden-skinned island flower.

"Keane and Marjorie will worry when they discover we arena at the Queen's Arms," Branwen said, her forehead puckered into a frown as she paused with her skirts raised, revealing tantalizingly turned ankles.

They'd fret far more when they learned Bryston had taken her aboard *The Dolphin*.

Nevertheless, that was precisely what he intended to do. He couldn't take a chance of Le Sauvage capturing her—torturing Branwen the way the rotter had Bryston's generous and trusting Delphine.

His stomach cramped as it always did when he thought of his dead wife—the vile, cruel way she'd died—and he ground his teeth together, causing his jaw to scream in protest.

What seemed an eternity later, his nerves and muscles taut and ears yet straining for a door crashing open, they reached the landing.

"Come on with ye." Abbie awaited them outside a chamber, the door open wide. She gestured curtly for them to enter ahead of her. A secretive smile bending her mouth, she again ran her curious gaze over Branwen as she led them into her personal boudoir.

Bryston had never been inside the madam's rooms before. Paintings of nudes in various intimate poses covered the walls in between gilded mirrors strategically placed to reflect the deep rose satin-covered mahogany four-poster bed dominating the room.

Branwen's astounded gaze traveled around the bedchamber, decorated in feminine shades of gold, pink, and ivory. Her mouth went slack when she spied the mirror positioned on the ceiling directly above the bed and several items laid upon a table, including silken scarves and a small whip.

Her questioning gaze flew to Bryston's, and he tried to pour reassurance into his.

Bloody hell, this is awkward.

Bringing an innocent into a well-seasoned prostitute's bedchamber. Never in all of Bryston's life had he ever considered he'd be in this situation.

Another knowing smirk bending her too-full mouth, Abbie directed them to a wall opposite the bed with a hidden panel ajar.

He, of course, knew the purpose of the voyeur's hidey-hole, but hoped to God that Branwen didn't.

His gut clenched again.

Keane would never forgive him for exposing her to this debauchery.

"In ye go, and dinna make a sound," the madam ordered, giving Branwen a small shove on her lower back. "Ye must remain absolutely silent," she warned.

A frown puzzling her brow, Branwen obediently stepped into the narrow closet-like room, not much larger than an armoire. A comfortable, gold velvet-covered, tufted bench took up most of the space.

"It will be a tight squeeze for the both of ye, especially given yer size, Captain." Abbie gave a bawdy wink, and her gaze turned speculative. "But the lass can always sit on yer lap."

Aye, she'd have to for them both to fit.

Branwen's jaw went slack again as she swung her attention between him and the bench.

He could almost hear the cogs in her mind grinding away.

Despite the perilousness of the situation, he chuckled in genuine amusement.

Branwen looked as if she'd been asked to don one of the strumpet's gowns and parade before their clientele below.

"Hurry up," Abbie snapped impatiently. "My regular client disna like bein' made to wait. And I dinna like him takin' his irritation out on me. Keep quiet too. He's no' one who likes peepers. He may refuse to pay me if he kens ye're here."

Branwen's eyes rounded impossibly larger. She scrambled

as far into the corner as she could manage as Bryston crouched down and wedged himself inside, shoving his sword to the side.

On second thought, an armoire was significantly larger than this inadequate cupboard.

A moment later, the panel clicked shut, and Abbie's footsteps faded as she left the chamber.

"Yer no' afraid of small spaces are ye?" Bryston suddenly thought to ask.

Too late if she was.

"Nae," Branwen whispered, her voice the veriest wisp of a sound. The insufficient space sucked the noise from the air.

With a soft grunt, he sank onto the bench, and without asking her permission, pulled her onto his lap. There was scarcely room to breathe in the compartment meant for one voyeur.

"Isna this cozy?" she muttered, sounding distinctly put upon and slightly breathy too. "There's more room in a whisky barrel."

"And ye'd know that, because...?"

He shouldn't, but he couldn't resist teasing her, even if he couldn't see her smile. Memory told him her smile made the silver flecks in her eyes sparkle and lit the room the way a full moon did the clear night sky.

"Dinna be flippant." She wiggled her bum, shifting first one way and then the other. "Ye ken what I mean. 'Tis mighty crowded in here, and yer dirk is diggin' into my side."

He pulled the offending weapon from his waist and laid it beside his thigh.

"Better?" he asked into her delicate ear.

"Aye." She sighed, the sound a breath of pent-up frustration and oddly forlorn. "How long do these things usually take?"

These...?

God's teeth. What a woman.

After choking back a laugh, he gritted his teeth against his body's immediate sexual response to her squirming bottom. The next several minutes very well might prove some of the most trying of his entire life.

Why the hell hadn't he considered this?

"It depends," he managed, pleased his voice sounded almost normal.

"On what?"

FIVE

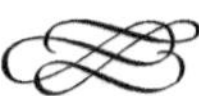

Sweet Jesus on the cross.

"'Tis nae a conversation I'll have with ye." Bryston flatly refused to discuss intercourse options with a virginal maid.

He'd always found Branwen attractive. Och, well, mayhap no' as an awkward lass, but assuredly he had since she'd become a woman fully grown. And until today, he'd never permitted himself a single unchaste thought about her.

Not only had his heart been too full of Delphine, but, as Keane's heavily protected ward, Branwen was off-limits. In truth, he'd been somewhat surprised the duke hadn't reacted more violently when Camden Kennedy had gone and married Bethea without permission.

Neither a coward nor a poltroon, Bryston wouldn't permit himself to contemplate Keane's reaction when he sailed to Le Havre with Branwen.

Not *The Dolphin's* original destination, but Bryston wanted to find De La Beche and learn if there were any truth to the treasure legend. Then perhaps he might rid himself of Le Sauvage and dispose of the piece of shite once and for all.

"I canna imagine what Keane and Marjorie will say when I

tell them where I've been," Branwen speculated, speaking her thoughts aloud.

She cautiously moved her head as if she peered into the darkness. The aroma of lavender and heather soap wafted from her silky hair as she brushed his chin with her crown.

Bryston gripped her shoulder, turning her to face him in the dim light. He could only make out the outline of her delicate features, but her scent wrapped around him like a woolen tartan.

A craving to settle his lips upon hers and explore the honeyed depths nearly choked him.

He swallowed hard and forced his desire down.

"Ye canna ever tell him, lass. Or her grace either. Nae one must ever ken."

"But why?"

He heard the frown in her melodious voice.

"Yer reputation would be ruined."

No sense in cushioning the truth. Branwen must understand the seriousness of her situation.

"Och, aye." She wilted against him. "That 'tis true for certain."

His knees nearly touching the door, he wrapped his arm around her waist and adjusted her. His cock perked to attention again at the unexpected friction, and he cursed inwardly. The last thing he needed was a cockstand pressing into Branwen Glanville's delectable rear end while a seasoned prostitute tended to her patron a scant few feet away.

What maggot had possessed him to seek shelter here?

Aye, his desire to save his and Branwen's lives.

Pray God, the gent wasn't the noisy sort, and that he and Abbie completed the act with relative haste.

Thin strips of light filtered into the chamber through the two peepholes, which Branwen had yet to notice. She had her profile to him, her eyes downcast as she fidgeted with her cloak.

"Ye'd best take your cloak off, lass. It will soon become too warm in here."

She cast him a sideways glance, then unfastened the clasps and let the thick mantle slide off her shoulders.

"I ken we're in a bordello, Bryston," she whispered. "But what is *this* place?"

God save him.

Not only for her outrageous curiosity but for the sound of his name upon her lips. An innocent verbal caress that should not have inflamed his desire but did.

What was it about Branwen Glanville that made him forget his vow to avoid feminine entanglements?

To forget Delphine?

Forget to guard his once mangled heart?

It came as an unwelcome start to realize his heart, though undeniably scarred, had healed.

Oh, it would never be whole, and life's experience had molded it into something far different than it had been five years before. Nevertheless, for some time now, every beat hadn't been an excruciating reminder he lived and breathed. And Delphine didn't.

And still, he wanted to bury his fingers in Branwen Glanville's hair and crush her mouth beneath his.

God. He sent a silent appeal heavenward.

Evidently, the Almighty heard his fervent prayer, for before he could answer Branwen's question, Abbie returned with her patron.

"Come on, Abbie, lass," a rough male voice pleaded. "Let me see those bonnie teats of yers that ye ken I'm so fond of. My wife's as flat-chested as an oatcake. I've missed yer full, ripe breasts, I have."

Branwen stiffened straighter than a freshly sawed board.

Bryston ran a soothing hand down her taut spine, wordlessly calming her.

Affront radiated off her in tangible waves.

Did she genuinely believe only unmarried males sought their pleasures in such places?

"My, yer in a hurry, Barday, arena ye?" The madam giggled before saying huskily, "Next time, dinna wait so long to visit me."

The man's response was lost as the unmistakable sound of noisy kissing and hurried disrobing commenced.

Bryston put a finger to Branwen's lips, signaling for her to remain silent.

She gave a slight nod and then, upon hearing "That's it, lass. Take me all the way into yer sweet mouth" followed by a gravelly moan, she buried her face in his neck and clamped her hands over her ears.

If only Bryston might do the same.

For God and all the saints help him, with this tantalizing wench straddling his thighs, her soft breasts pushing into his chest, and her warm breath teasing his throat—not to mention the unmistakable, guttural sounds of joining taking place upon the bed—he was nigh onto spilling his seed where he sat.

He closed his eyes, clamped his teeth together, and rested his head against the back of the closet.

Think of somethin' else. Anythin' else, Bryston commanded himself, as his member pulsed painfully, thickening against his will.

Scurvy aboard my ship.

Le Sauvage and his dogs.

Delphine.

"Och, Abbie. Aye. Aye," the man moaned throatily.

He knew exactly when Branwen felt his rigid length nudging her delectable bum.

She raised her head, peering at him, then quite deliberately ground the plump twin mounds of her bottom into his groin as if to say "Behave, ye unconscionable bounder."

If only he could, but his cock was a randy, intractable thing, and it sensed a woman's glorious heat was nearby. And, it reminded him, quite audaciously, that it hadn't experienced a release in a woman's sweet body in a long, long—*too long*—while.

Nae since Delphine's death.

Praise the divine powers, he couldn't clearly see Branwen's expression.

His member pulsed again.

Dammit.

He wasn't a callow youth about to bed his first woman.

Bryston felt her swift inhalation and feared Branwen was about to scold him when the outer chamber door crashed open. It opened with such force that the door reverberated off the wall and shattered a mirror.

Abbie screeched, and her partner bellowed his outrage.

SIX

Just as Branwen was about to throw caution and good sense to the four corners and demand Bryston control his lustful urges, someone stormed into the bedchamber. After all, how was she supposed to ignore something that size and hard flexing against her bottom?

She clutched his shoulders, digging her nails into the rippling muscles, going cold as fear streaked through her and set her to trembling uncontrollably.

Bryston drew her to his chest, running his hands up and down her spine comfortingly. He pressed his warm lips to her ear and whispered very quietly, "Shh."

She shuddered but wasn't altogether positive fear was the sole cause. His touch did strange things to her. Heightened her senses and made her aware of every breath he took, the sensual caress of his fingers on her back, his shallow breaths, and that glorious mouth mere inches from hers.

Men's lips weren't supposed to be so appealing.

If she but angled her head the merest bit...

"How dare ye interrupt me when I'm entertainin' a

guest?" Abbie's shrill voice could've peeled wallpaper from the walls. "Git yerself downstairs and wait yer turn."

She put on a performance that would've done a professional actress credit.

"*Unless*...ye want to join us, that is." Her voice turned coy. "Yer a braw mon. I could do somethin' verra, *verra* special with those feathers in yer hat," she purred.

Good Lord and all the saints.

All sorts of images sprang to mind, and a nervous giggle bubbled up Branwen's throat. Shoulders quaking, she bit the inside of her mouth and crammed her face into Bryston's thick neck.

He smelled of leather and pine trees and his own musky scent.

She struggled to control her laughter.

They might hear her.

She *must* remain silent.

Bryston squeezed her in silent warning, and she nodded against his thick throat, drawing his essence deep into her lungs.

"Or, perhaps ye'd like to have a seat yonder by the armoire and watch?" Mockery tinged Abbie's invitation. "Ye'd still have to pay the usual fee, mind ye, but I vow I'll make it worth yer while."

"I dinna want to share ye, Abbie," Barday whined. "And ye ken, I dinna like an audience."

Och, who in God's holy name would?

"Never ye mind, dearie." What sounded like a slap to a backside echoed in the room. "Abbie kens how to please more than one man. I promise ye, ye'll have nae complaints when I'm finished with ye."

Two men.

At once?

Was that even possible?

Branwen's brain cramped, trying to envision such a thing.

And what, exactly, did the abbess mean by watching?

Branwen squinted at the door, noting for the first time a pair of small holes strategically placed where someone might look through them. In that instant, she understood just the manner of compartment she and Bryston hid inside. She might be naive, but she wasn't dimwitted.

Mortification and heat surged from her waist to her hairline.

"Come on, then, love." The bed squeaked in protest, as Abbie must've adjusted her position to accommodate the intruder. "I've made room for ye. Do ye have a name?"

"*Non*," came a revulsion-ridden French male voice. "I'm seeking *mon ami*. 'Tis urgent that I find him. He's tall, blond, and has a scar on his face, just here."

It *was* the Frenchman who'd been chasing them.

Branwen went hot then cold, then heat and moisture sprang out upon her forehead.

If Bryston hadn't had the forethought to hide—

Branwen curled her fingers into his broad shoulders, and he pressed his warm mouth to her ear again. He didn't speak, but she knew he urged her to remain silent.

"Och, now do ye see any tall blonds here?" The bed squeaked again. "I canna say that I've seen any mon matchin' that description either."

The sound of heavy footsteps on first the wood floor and then muffled on the thick carpet carried to the closet.

"*What* do ye think ye're doin'?" Abbie asked, her voice rising half an octave in offended affront.

"Looking beneath your bed and in your armoire, mademoiselle, *oui*?" A disappointed grunt followed the clacking of the wardrobe's doors banging shut.

"I told ye, nae one was here, *monsieur*." She spat the last word, making it sound like a foul oath. "And if the man ye seek is yer friend, why would he be hidin' beneath my bed or in my wardrobe?"

"Dammit, Abbie. All this jabberin' caused me to lose my cockstand," Barday complained, and the bed groaned again.

Branwen guessed he'd arisen. She bloody well wasn't looking through those two convenient holes. She was afraid of what she might see.

"I'm nae payin' for yer favors when I didna even come," Barday whined, very much sounding like a laddie denied a bonbon.

"See what ye've done now, *Frangach*?" Abbie cried sullenly, addressing the Frenchman in Gaelic. "Ye can pay his fee since ye interrupted us. That will be two pounds."

"*Mon Dieu, non*. I *never* pay for whores, and certainly not two pounds for a fat *putain* far past her prime." A scornful laugh filled the chamber, and Branwen shuddered.

Bryston's enemy was an evil man.

"Get out, ye bastard, before I call the bouncers." Every trace of seductiveness had left Abbie's tone, and only smoldering fury weighted each cracking syllable.

"With pleasure." The rhythmic click of booted footsteps retreating faded, followed by a sharp whistle. "Bisonette, Faucheux, search every room, even the kitchen. *Zut*, the tavern keeper down the street swears he saw a man matching McPherson's description enter this building."

Branwen uncoiled her fingers from where she'd been gripping Bryston's arms and drew in her first real breath in the past ten minutes.

"I'm sorry, Barday," Abbie cajoled in soothing tones. "Are ye positive ye dinna want to finish?"

"Nae. I'm limper than my wife's tattie scones." He grunted, and a couple of thuds followed.

Had he donned his boots?

"Dinna look so sad, lass. Yer nae fat. I adore yer generous curves."

Branwen pressed her lips tight, resisting the urge to cover her ears again. There was something so wrong about listening to such intimacies.

"Yer a love, Barday," Abbie said with something that sounded like real affection.

"I wish my wife thought so." Still grumbling beneath his breath, he shuffled from the room.

Several long moments passed, and Branwen supposed the woman was dressing. She gave a small start when Abbie whispered outside the closet. "Stay put until I've made sure they've left."

As if they had any choice.

Did this chamber even have a method of opening from the inside?

Branwen slouched against Bryston, all of her energy sapped at once.

How much time had passed since she'd left Holyrood Abbey?

Were Keane and Marjorie at the Queen's Arms wondering where she was?

She must go to them at once.

"Ye did well, lass," Bryston whispered against her cheek. "I'm verra proud of ye."

"I was terrified," she murmured low and shifted, turning her face toward the door. "This closet is for someone to watch a couple joinin' on the bed, isna it? Why would anyone want to do that?"

SEVEN

Lucky Spence's House

Bryston had _no_ intention of explaining peculiar sexual preferences or fetishes to the innocent woman perched upon his lap. Instead, he directed her attention to their escape. "Once Abbie verifies Le Sauvage has indeed departed, we'll need to don a disguise and slip out."

He wouldn't tell her their destination was still his ship because he hadn't a single doubt she'd strenuously object, and he wasn't in the mood to bargain with her. Precisely how he and Branwen would board the vessel undetected, he'd yet to work out.

Hopefully, Zhao and Bayu had deduced what had occurred and were already aboard _The Dolphin,_ awaiting him and ready to weigh anchor at a moment's notice. If he didn't hurry, however, he'd miss the tide, and he didn't relish trying to fend off Le Sauvage and his men until the next.

Astute and intelligent, Keane would surmise what he needed to do to keep his family safe, and Bryston knew full well that didn't include loitering at the Queen's Arms.

The duke would return to Edinburgh and await word about Branwen at Parkhill Hall, where his clansmen could guard him and his new wife and stepdaughters. After what Keane had just undergone with his other ward, Bryston didn't want to contemplate the wrath that would be directed toward him when he didn't return Branwen directly to her guardian's safekeeping.

To do so, however, would put Keane and his family in untold danger. He didn't know to what extent of a peril Le Sauvage presented, nor why he'd appeared after all of this time. But as the first words from the bastard's mouth had been a threat against Branwen, Bryston could only assume the worst.

Nae, by taking Branwen with him aboard *The Dolphin*, he could lure the wily spawn of Satan away. Undoubtedly, that course involved risk—a great deal of risk—but it was a chance he'd have to take.

What other recourse had he?

Le Sauvage wrongly assumed Branwen was Bryston's woman, which put her life in tremendous peril. Where he'd arrived at such a misconception, Bryston couldn't imagine.

"Bryston?" Branwen murmured. "Why is the Frenchman after ye, and why disna anyone ken ye were married?"

Once more, unsurprisingly, Branwen came directly to the point.

Head cocked, listening for Abbie's return, he returned in a low tenor, "I'll tell ye all, lass, but no' right now. I dinna want to take a chance Le Sauvage or his men are loiterin' outside. Stay quiet until Abbie assures us they've gone."

Her silky hair brushed his chin as she nodded, and a whiff of her unique lavender and heather scent floated about them. She smelled of spring and the Highlands and her own tantalizing, womanly essence.

He breathed her in, inhaling her fragrance deep into his

lungs, yearning to explore her satiny skin, to discover if she smelled of heather and lavender everywhere. If her skin was as velvety soft and impossibly creamy as her face and neck.

Careful! A warning pealed in his head and heart. *Ye ken what happened the last time ye cared for a woman.*

Cared for a woman?

He didn't *care* for Branwen Glanville. Yet even as the denial resounded in his mind, he knew it for the colossal lie that it was.

Not more than a score of heartbeats later, the distinct click of the outer door shutting and the lock turning carried to him, and then Abbie opened the panel.

"Hurry with ye." She motioned to the bed. "I've collected cloaks and bonnets to disguise ye. My girls are watchin' the streets, and three of us will accompany ye." She eyed Branwen as she stood and stepped from the closet. "Aye, I guessed yer size accurately."

"My size?" Branwen sent him a bewildered frown.

"Ye canna hope to escape in that fancy thing ye were wearin'. 'Tis a beacon, callin' attention to ye." Abbie held out a dove-gray cloak. "This is for ye, and so is the bonnet." She indicted a matching veiled cap atop the satin coverlet.

"Thank ye," Branwen said as she accepted the humble garment and draped it around her shoulders without complaint. Undoubtedly, she knew it belonged to one of the prostitutes, yet she voiced no objection.

Stifling a groan as blood returned to his legs, Bryston collected his dirk, unfolded from the bench, and ducked beneath the doorframe. He held Branwen's expensive velvet mantle as he slid his dirk back into his waistband.

"And *these* are for ye, Captain."

Abbie grinned, a wicked glint in her amused gaze. She extended an ugly as sin black cloak, but it was the hat that captured his disbelieving gaze. An atrocious, oversized straw thing with a thick black veil.

"Nae one will believe I'm a woman, Abbie," he grumbled as he dropped Branwen's cloak onto the rumpled bed before accepting the garment the madam held out to him.

She arched a skeptical brow. "Nae? I've two lasses who are nearly six feet tall, Captain, and neither is trim of form. They'll be accompanyin' us. They said it sounded like a fun adventure." Her mouth slanted saucily as she leaned near Branwen and said conspiratorially, "Some men like a woman to dominate them in bed."

Once more, Branwen's pretty mouth sagged. Her eyes wide with astonishment, her gaze searched Bryston's, a question in its depths.

He shut his eyes, cringing at having to explain *that* to her, for he had no doubt the curious minx would ask at the first opportunity. He didn't think she'd forgotten he hadn't answered her question about the purpose of the voyeur's closet either. Or what determined how long a joining took.

Abbie pointed at the ghastly hat, more suitable for a funeral a decade past than anything a lady of the night might wear. "Ye help him with the bonnet, lass, while I fetch my cloak. Ye'll need to slouch and hunch yer shoulders, Captain."

"Abbie, ye canna go with us," Bryston objected, but she was already rifling through her wardrobe. "'Tis dangerous."

"Aye, I can. Ye see, Captain, ye picked a good day to visit." She plopped a frightening purple bonnet atop her red hair. "Every Saturday afternoon, several of the lasses and I don our cloaks and veiled hats—lest we offend the *genteel* folk of Leith —and we go shoppin'."

Planting her hands on her ample hips, she grinned.

Bryston was still convinced he'd stick out like a crow amidst doves, but he didn't have a better plan. If Abbie and her lasses could provide a distraction, he might just be able to sweep Branwen aboard his ship. Especially if his men could contribute to the commotion.

A plan began to form, and he skewed his lips sideways.

Aye, that would do.

She winked at Branwen. "Even the likes of us appreciates a pretty ribbon, a new fan, scented soap, or some fallall or other."

"Thank ye for yer help and the cloak and bonnet." Branwen offered a friendly smile. "I am verra grateful."

No judgment or censure colored her words.

Approval lit the madam's eyes.

By not acting haughty or superior, Branwen had guaranteed Abbie's silence.

"Abbie, do ye have a lad who runs errands for ye?" Bryston asked.

Fastening her cloak, she glanced up. "Aye."

"I want him to deliver a message to *The Dolphin* for me." He offered a crooked grin. "My crew can help provide a spectacle if yer lasses dinna mind puttin' on a performance of their own."

She tossed her head back and squared her shoulders. "My girls put on brilliant performances every day, ye well ken."

Aye, bedding every sort of man and pretending to enjoy themselves. It was a hard life, and he'd never judged the women but felt compassion for their lot.

"*The Dolphin?*" Branwen's raven eyebrows stitched together, and the corners of her eyes crinkled. "Why no' the Queen's Arms?"

Bloody hell.

"Branwen...?" Bryston scraped a hand through his hair.

After clearing her throat, Abbie said, "I'll just fetch those writin' supplies for ye, Captain."

"Bryston? Why arena we going' to the tavern? Keane and Marjorie will be waitin' for me."

He eased the offensive bonnet from her grasp and tossed it on the bed. Taking her cold hands in his, he gave them a little squeeze. "Lass, they'll no' be there. My men will have told them about Le Sauvage, and the duke will have wisely taken his family and returned to Edinburgh."

"I think ye need to tell me precisely what is goin' on." She wrinkled her pert nose, puzzlement making three neat lines on her smooth forehead. She folded her arms in that stubborn way that was so Branwen and jutted her chin out in an endearingly mulish manner. "Especially if ye think to take me aboard yer ship willin'ly."

She had a right to know because her life was still in peril.

Blowing out a long breath, he cupped his nape. "Strikin' a bargain, are ye lass?"

She rolled her shoulder as she cast an apprehensive glance to the window, then the door. "Nae, I dinna bargain with a Highland buccaneer. But I would have the truth. I've found honesty saves a great deal of trouble in the end."

He advanced to the gold velvet-festooned window. After edging the curtain aside and seeing no sign of Le Sauvage or his henchmen, he nodded.

"Marc-André Chastain, or Le Sauvage, as he's dubbed himself, is a pirate. Not a privateer, but a foul, vicious, bloodthirsty, unmerciful pirate. A scourge and a bane on humanity."

She paled slightly but pursed her mouth and gave a nod for him to continue.

"He erroneously became convinced my wife knew the location of a hidden treasure. Delphine's mother had been a *Filles du Roi*, sent by the French government to Tortuga to become a wife to a male colonist."

"Women did that? Married complete strangers?" Branwen asked, paler now and undeniably appalled at the notion.

"Aye. For a few years on various French colonies." He lifted the travesty of a hat and plopped the wretched thing upon his head. *Hideous.* He couldn't prevent his grimace. Was there ever an uglier woman than he?

"When her tavern keeper husband died, Anne Foissey took over runnin' his saloon. Not long afterward, she became lovers with a privateer, Mical De La Beche. According to what Anne told Delphine, he fathered her."

"Ye must've loved yer wife verra much to name yer ship after her." Compassion softened the angles of her face and the corners of her eyes. "Her second name was Rose, I take it?"

Her gaze drifted to his right arm, though his clothing covered the tattoo.

So, the lass had seen his tattoo, had she?

Interesting.

Had she watched him as he trained?

"Aye," he said gruffly, remembered grief constricting his throat. He'd vowed to never experience the pain her death had caused him again.

If his heart had been carved from his chest with a letter opener and then diced into pieces, the pain would've been trifling compared to seeing how Delphine had suffered from Le Sauvage's cruel viciousness.

He fumbled with the bonnet's double ribbons until Branwen shoved his hands aside and, after adjusting the hat, tied the black ribbons into a jaunty bow to the side of his chin. When she eyed the finished product, her mouth quivered, but she schooled her mirth.

"Why is this Le Sauvage scunner after ye?" she asked gently.

Bryston glanced into one of the looking glasses, amused at

the big, homely woman staring back at him. Not even an ape-drunk tippler straight off a ship at sea for six months would mistake him for a female.

How much should he tell Branwen?

Everything, he decided with a final grimace at the black-clad creature in the reflection.

"For over two decades, Anne swore to anyone who'd listen to her drunken ravin's that De La Beche had told her about a massive treasure he'd hidden, acquired from a decade of plunderin's. He also said he'd return to Tortuga and take her back to France with him, which, of course, he never did. The man was a charlatan and a liar, and I'm convinced nae treasure ever existed. He'd simply wanted to wheedle his way into her bed."

"How did ye meet yer wife?" A blush bloomed across Branwen's face, but she didn't look away.

"She was tendin' bar when my ship put into port five years ago. Her mother had died six months before, but the legend of De La Beche's treasure lived on. Delphine vowed it was a fanciful tale that grew into a legend as time passed, and it was repeated and embellished with each tellin'."

Unlike her mother, his wife had operated a respectable establishment—as respectable as one could be on an island known for sequestering all manner of swashbucklers, buccaneers, and pirates, in addition to mercenaries and prostitutes.

He twisted his mouth into a wry smile. Delphine had four gargantuan bouncers who tossed anyone out on their arses the minute they looked sideways at her. She was adored by one and all for her kindness and generosity.

Anne had been a drunkard and braggart, but she'd raised an intelligent, independent daughter, and Bryston had fallen half in love with her that sunny afternoon she'd slammed that first tankard of warm, dark ale on the table before him.

"And this Le Sauvage heard about the treasure and...?" Branwen probed.

He'd have to give her credit for her tenacity. And bravery too. She hadn't succumbed to tears or histrionics, and her fortitude was praiseworthy.

"Bryston?"

Closing his eyes, he braced himself as the memories of that godawful day crashed over him like a gigantic, unmerciful wave. "He tried to torture the truth from her. She couldna tell him what she dinna ken. He gave me this." He flicked his fingers toward the scar on his face. "And he left us both for dead when my crew arrived and drove him and his men off."

"I am verra sorry, Bryston." She touched his forearm, a sheen of moisture making her eyes glassy. "But why is he after ye now, after all of this time?"

"That, I dinna ken. But what I do ken, is he believes ye're my woman." He met her silver gaze, realizing with a start that navy-blue ringed the gray. "And that means I canna let ye out of my sight. Ye must sail to France with me."

"Good Lord and all the saints." Her features crumpled in astonishment. "Why would he think such a thing? Is he daft?"

"Aye, he's mad. Off his head." A stark-raving lunatic.

Loudly clearing her throat, Abbie re-entered her bedchamber with the writing implements. "Here ye go, now."

In short order, Bryston penned a brief missive to Zhao. The Chinaman had a mischievous streak and a particular fondness for fireworks. A combination that worked well for what Bryston intended.

He also wrote Keane a letter. He lifted the folded rectangle after affixing the wax seal. "This is for Roxdale, Abbie. It explains we're sailin' to France but will be back within a month."

"*A month?*" Branwen blanched and swallowed. "A

month?" she repeated, unable to keep the dismay from her voice. "That long?"

"Aye. Yer family would be in peril if ye returned to them before I deal with Le Sauvage once and for all." Bryston lowered the hat's veil and slouched as Abbie had recommended.

"But it disna take a month to sail to France and back," Branwen insisted, glancing at Abbie and then back to him.

"Nae, but it may take me that long to find De La Beche. *If* he yet lives, that is."

And if he didn't? Then what?

God's bollocks, Bryston didn't bloody well know.

Abbie looked on, sympathy brimming in her eyes. She also knew what this meant for Branwen. How many of the women in this whorehouse had been compromised through no fault of their own, and their only recourse afterward had been to sell their bodies?

At least Branwen had her family, which included a powerful, wealthy duke as her guardian. Unlike Camden Kennedy, who'd salvaged Bethea Glanville's reputation by marrying her, Bryston wouldn't make the same noble sacrifice.

He'd known true love and vowed the day Delphine had been ripped from his life—taking his heart, soul, and joy with her to the grave—that he'd never wed again. Loving another was out of the question. He was a man who loved but once in a lifetime.

No remorse speared him. He'd save Branwen's and possibly Roxdale's and his family's lives. That was enough, and if the duke or anyone else expected more, hoped for more— well, disappointment was in their futures.

"Yer point is well taken. I willna knowin'ly put my family in danger." Giving a brusque nod, Branwen turned toward the door. "Shall we go?"

Again, her stalwartness and pragmatism impressed him. Her acceptance of the situation earned further respect. Branwen Glanville was a singularly remarkable woman.

As they departed the chamber, Abbie chuckled. "Just wait until ye see what the lasses and I have planned."

Somehow, Bryston didn't doubt it would be utterly scandalous, and he prayed to God that it would carve enough time for his and Branwen's escape.

Fifteen minutes later, having walked to the wharf unmolested, Bryston, Branwen, and the four prostitutes, as well as two of Lucky Spence's more intimidating bouncers, stood in an alley adjacent to the docks. *The Dolphin* swayed in the harbor, her colorful flag fluttering flirtatiously in the everpresent breeze.

Squinting from behind the lacy veil covering his face, Bryston grinned. Zhao and another four of Bryston's crew wheeled an innocuous cart, no different than a dozen or so others, toward the middle of the dockyard.

He didn't know precisely what Abbie and her girls had planned, but he was positive it was something that would draw keen attention.

"Are ye ready, lasses?" Bryston asked the demurely attired women.

"Aye," they chorused, then giggled as if privy to a great secret.

He touched Abbie's arm before passing her a weighty purse. "Thank ye, Abbie. I'll send ye more."

"Nae need, Captain." Shaking her head, she accepted the coins and tucked them inside a pocket concealed within her skirts. "Ye always treated the lasses and me with respect. That's worth more than ye'll ever ken. And yer lady is a kindhearted lass too."

My lady?

Before he could correct her assumption, she turned and sauntered onto the gray-brown planking. "Ye ken what to do, dearies."

A moment later, having shed their conservative hats and cloaks to reveal scandalous gowns, the women paraded forth, advertising their assets with the confidence of those well-practiced in the profession. At once, they drew loud whistles and hoots from the myriad of men on the docks for one reason or another.

Laborers, merchants, and sailors paused in their tasks, their attention riveted on the women flashing lengths of pale legs and tantalizing glimpses of creamy shoulders and bosoms.

"They really are somethin'," Branwen said, admiration inflecting her voice rather than derision or condemnation. "I admire their confidence."

Well, that was one way to describe their behavior.

As the women posed and preened, even blowing flirtatious kisses to the bystanders, his crew casually glanced around. Two of his men unconcernedly tucked their hands into their pockets, another pair nonchalantly hefted coils of rope over their shoulders, and Zhao lit his clay pipe as if he didn't have a care in the world.

Bryston's first mate and *The Dolphin's* captain in his absence, Zhao glanced around, then slipped the pipe beneath the tarp covering the cart's contents. The other men exchanged pointed looks before picking up their paces and moving swiftly away.

Bryston wrapped his hand around Branwen's upper arm and edged them out of the alley and along the weatherworn grayish building to their left.

"When I tell ye to, lass, run for all yer worth and follow Zhao. He'll have a boat waitin' to row out to *The Dolphin.*

Dinna wait for me if we are separated. Board that skiff, and they'll transport ye to my ship and keep ye safe."

He'd no sooner finished speaking when the contents of the cart erupted. Earsplitting fireworks exploded, launching high into the sky. The wharf vibrated, men roared, women screamed, and he and Branwen sprinted across the rough timbers.

The goddamn hat bobbed wildly atop his head, and the veil obstructed his vision.

How in the hell did women manage while draped in these trappings all the time?

As Bryston ran, guarding Branwen with his body, he waited for a lead ball to rip into him or for Le Sauvage and his men to confront them with blades at the ready.

Glancing over his shoulder, he swore as his nemesis stormed around the corner, leading his men. The two men he'd spied with him earlier led the pack. Fury narrowed his eyes and rage nearly blinded him when he recognized a Highlander he'd seen a few times during the Hogmanay celebration at Trentwick Castle last December.

A bloody, damned spy.

That must be where Le Sauvage received the misinformation about Bryston and Branwen. True, they had shared a dance, and if he recalled, he'd been seated beside her at least thrice during supper. The latter had been by chance and not ploy.

Shite.

"*Allez au diable*, McPherson!" bellowed the Frenchman.

Damn ye too, ye buggering whoremonger.

Abbie placed two fingers in her mouth and let out a high-pitched whistle. Without hesitation, she and her girls flipped their skirts up over their backs, baring their naked behinds.

They wiggled their bottoms suggestively before dissolving into laughter and running off.

Thank God, Branwen hadn't seen *that* display.

Several eager men charged after the women, cutting off Le Sauvage's pursuit.

Heart thundering between his ears as loudly as the earlier bang, he handed Branwen into the skiff. Another explosion flared, sparks flying high into the sky, as he and his crew rowed him and Branwen to the relative safety of his ship.

Och, now the real game begins.

EIGHT

19 April 1721
Early Morning
Strait of Dover

Branwen wrapped the borrowed cloak around her snugger as she shifted her gaze between the white cliffs of Dover, England on the starboard and France to the vessel's port side. On this brilliantly clear morning, the sun caused the Strait of Dover, as Bryston had called the waterway, to twinkle and sparkle as *The Dolphin* sailed the last stretch of their journey to Le Havre, France.

Deep cobalt in the middle of the channel, the tapestry of waters became gradually lighter shades of blue nearer to the shore due to the chalky cliffs shedding into the coastline.

The ship moved as gracefully as any dancer, neatly dividing the sea, her snapping sails proud and full as she unerringly carried them forward.

A dozen men moved about the deck of the sleek schooner in what Branwen had come to recognize as their morning routine. Everything aboard *The Dolphin* bespoke discipline and order, and the men's loyalty and devotion to their captain was commendable.

Surprisingly, for a group of former privateers, given the superstitions she'd heard about women being bad luck aboard a vessel, the sailors had accepted her presence with little more than a raised bristly eyebrow, a calloused hand scrubbed across a stubbly chin, or a furrowed craggy forehead.

Evidently, their confidence in Bryston made her company acceptable, even if she was female. She suspected, however, he'd also spoken to them that first night, and though she had no notion what he might've said, there hadn't been a single uncomfortable incident.

No scowls, glowers, mutters, cold shoulders—nothing.

Abbie had mistakenly assumed she was Bryston's woman. Perhaps his crew had as well.

In truth, she wasn't positive how that inaccurate assumption made her feel. Part of her thrilled at being his, and another part was appalled that people could so readily believe them a couple.

Face raised, Branwen inhaled the tangy air and smiled as several fulmars, their black-tipped wings stiff and outstretched, glided gracefully through the air. The seabirds didn't make a sound as they dove and swooped above the frolicking waves.

She loved this.

Adored the morning as the day began on the ship. Loved the spray on her face, the feel of the wind in her hair, which she'd left down and now fluttered about her shoulders and back. The sounds, the smells, admiring the sunrise and sunset from the poop deck—all of it.

Except for the lack of a bathtub.

There wasn't one aboard the ship, and Branwen longed for a good soak and to scrub her salt-laden hair. The daily wash with warm water from a bucket was welcome but nowhere near as satisfying as a real bath.

Her tummy hadn't rebelled at the unaccustomed rising and dipping of the ocean as she'd expected either. It did contract, however, and a sick sensation flopped about her middle every time she pondered how Keane and Marjorie had reacted upon receiving Bryston's letter. Likely Bethea didn't know what had happened yet, and that was one small thing for which Branwen was grateful.

She'd ask to write to them as soon as they landed in France.

Nevertheless, she couldn't help but fret that Keane and Marjorie worried about her wellbeing, and they needn't do so.

Once safe from the raving lunatic chasing Bryston, she'd been treated with the utmost courtesy. And though she ought to be wary of the former buccaneer crew, she was not.

In fact, she quite liked the motley array of seamen with their tattoos and piercings, colorful language, lilting accents, and often bizarre attire. They were a rough, uncouth, burly lot, and while Branwen wasn't naive enough to believe them harmless—for each wore multiple weapons upon his scarred person—they fascinated her.

Oh, the glorious tales and wondrous adventures they'd shared with her this past week. Such grand escapades to so many exotic and thrilling places. Naturally, they didn't share the seedier side of being reformed privateers, but the stories they'd woven created such a grand tapestry in her mind. She could almost see the fascinating places they described.

Zhao was Bryston's first mate and the fourth son of a Chinese nobleman who'd fled home at sixteen before being forced into an arranged marriage. Next to Bryston, he was the most serious of the lot. Bayu, only marginally less somber, was a Sumatran. He told her of his home and a delightful myth about the Tiger People of the forest.

Jabir, a hulking giant of a man from Morocco, had beautiful nut-brown skin, a deep, lyrical voice, and a contagious laugh that boomed across the ocean. Scags—surely not his real name—a tall, rickle-a-bones Scot, was a genuinely gifted fiddler, and Connolly, the ship's medical officer, was a bespectacled, scholarly man with perhaps more affection for rum than was wise.

They were a rough and coarse conglomeration of cast-offs, but together they seemed more of an irregular family of misfits than mere crewmembers. And that they were delighted their captain sailed with them on this journey was as evident as the black leather patch over Scags' right eye.

They revered, respected, and, aye, loved their captain.

As Branwen had observed him this past week, she'd come to know a Bryston McPherson she'd never had the privilege of knowing on land. If any man was born to captain a ship, it was him. He held his men in real affection, and his laugh rang out frequently as he jested and joked with them.

More than once—*fine, several times*—she'd covertly watched him at the helm, legs splayed, broad shoulders back, and face forward as he marked the ship's progress. The lines of tension eased around the corners of his handsome face, and a sparkle shone in the depths of his eyes that was missing when he was on land.

So why had he left the sea when he so obviously loved her? Relished this way of life?

A fulmar circled back to Branwen, looking her straight in the eye for several seconds before winging away. It swooped low over the frothing water, and as it rose, a half dozen silvery white-beaked dolphins jumped beside the ship.

A cry went up from the crewman who'd spotted the animals too.

"Dolphins on the starboard side," came the shout from high above her. That would be Edmunds, the cabin boy and rigging monkey, clinging to the mast.

"Aye, 'tis a good omen," Scags said, in his thick as cold molasses brogue.

An epiphany struck Branwen with such intensity that she knew she'd accidentally stumbled upon the truth.

His wife's death.

Delphine—French for dolphin.

That was why Bryston stopped captaining *The Dolphin*. A vessel named after his beloved wife, a woman he'd loved so much. He couldn't continue sailing after she'd died so tragically.

Did he blame himself for her death?

That he couldn't stop Le Sauvage in time?

Curling her lips inward over her teeth, Branwen pondered that, then nodded to herself.

Quite possibly, and with Le Sauvage back from the dead, everything Bryston had tried to put behind him, to forget, was once more guiding his life. Very much like the wind in the ship's sails sped them onward, even now.

Aye, but a good sailor knew how to use the wind and sails to take him where he wanted to go. However, she highly doubted Bryston had as much control over his life—or hers, for that matter—right now.

The wind played with her hair, flinging a few strands across her face. She brushed them aside, wincing slightly at their stiff texture. No small surprise, her hair was dirty and in need of washing after nearly a week at sea.

She'd lost the bonnet Abbie had given her in the mad dash to the skiff, and the cloak didn't have a hood.

Rather than sail directly to France, Bryston had lingered in the North Sea for several days to throw Le Sauvage off their trail. When they reached Le Havre, he intended to try to find De La Beche and put the hidden treasure myth to rest once and for all.

She wasn't confident that would do any good or, in truth, if it were possible. If Le Sauvage was as crazed as Bryston said he was, the pirate mightn't believe the priceless plunder didn't exist, even if De La Beche told him so himself.

What then?

She shuddered, acute fear for Bryston sending a chill winging through her.

He despised Le Sauvage, rightly so, and she didn't believe he'd ever be at peace until the pirate no longer breathed.

"Good mornin' to ye, lass." As he so often did, Bryston had silently approached her as she stood before the rail at the ship's bow. How such a large man could move so stealthily baffled her. "Did ye sleep well?"

Nae, she'd not slept well a single night, but she'd not tell him that.

Especially after he'd insisted she occupy his cabin, the door of which boasted a stout bolt to deter any unwanted visitors. He'd bunked with his crew, and she was both relieved and chagrined that he'd relinquished his quarters so that she might be comfortable and safe.

His face sun-bronzed, his hair tied back in a queue, he wore what she'd come to understand was his typical attire aboard ship. Black breeches, knee-high boots, a linen shirt open at the neck, a wide black belt at his waist from whence his dirk protruded, and the crimson scarf knotted at his throat. Today, his sword was also in place at his hip, again reminding her they'd reach their destination in a matter of hours.

He passed her a steaming cup of strong tea, which she gratefully accepted. That, too, had become a routine this past week. After her morning ablutions, she'd come above deck and greet the new day, enjoy a cup of tea with him, and then eat a simple but filling breakfast of oat porridge, oatcakes, ham, and all the strong tea or coffee she could wish for.

She wished for tea.

Bryston preferred coffee, and she suspected something a wee bit stronger frequently laced his beverage.

Bryston's attention lingered on her mouth, and she automatically trailed her tongue across her bottom lip to catch any droplets of tea that might remain there.

His facial muscles tensed, and his eyelids slammed shut for a long blink. He'd done that often of late, and Branwen couldn't help but wonder if he wanted to kiss her.

Did she want him to?

Aye, verra much.

"Branwen?" he inquired, a dark blond eyebrow cocked.

What had he asked?

Aye, how had she slept?

"I slept well enough, though I confess to a wee bit of a waffy stomach durin' the night."

She shifted her gaze to the shoreline once more, and a tremor skittered up her spine, spreading out across her shoulders.

Were they headed to safety or into a trap?

Would La Sauvage await them, bold and brazenly, when they went ashore? Or would he slither around, hiding in fusty nooks, hoping for an opportunity to strike? Or had he sailed to warmer climes since *The Dolphin* was to have sailed to the Caribbean?

She fervently prayed the latter.

The ship would still voyage to the Caribbean, but only after Bryston had returned Branwen to Scotland. Or so he'd said.

Branwen guessed that was what Bryston hoped had happened. That the scurrilous bounder had voyaged to the tropics. It would give him plenty of time to locate Mical De La Beche, *if* he yet lived.

If not...

Well, she didn't know what Bryston intended then. He'd not spoken of an alternative plan.

She supposed he'd return her to the bosom of her family, but what would *he* do?

Her stomach wobbled in the queer way it had the past few days when she thought of not seeing Bryston every day. She'd come to like and admire him a great deal. More than was wise, an inner voice warned, not for the first time.

Bryston took a long swallow from his mug and gave a satisfied sigh. "I'm sorry ye dinna feel well. The sea grew rough for a wee spell. I should've checked on ye."

"There was nae need. Nerves about arrivin' in Le Havre today, no' the seas, caused the upset. I'm perfectly fine now. Honestly, I am." His keen, slightly narrowed gaze probed behind her falsely cheerful declaration, and she blurted, "Did ye see the dolphins?"

Something flashed across his face—Pain? Guilt? Regret? Sorrow?—and she immediately regretted her impulsiveness.

Damn my quick tongue.

"I envy ye, Bryston." She swept her gaze across the ocean. A mere week on the sea and she'd miss it when she returned to the Highlands. "The places ye've visited and will in the future. The freedom ye have." Shaking her head, causing her hair to swirl around her, she gave a self-conscious laugh. "Women dinna have such opportunities."

He stepped closer, his large body shielding her from the curious stares of his crew. "Branwen?"

A note in the timbre of his voice caused her heartbeat to falter, stall, and then gallop forward much like an unrestrained racehorse.

She tilted her head, taking in the whiskers shadowing his strong jawline, and the concern in his dark brown eyes framed by lashes the same color, though they were gold-tipped. Fine lines etched the corners of his eyes, and her attention strayed to the scar marring his cheek.

Before she contemplated what she was doing, she traced its rough length with two fingertips. "I canna look upon this without a pang in my heart for the pain ye suffered."

The words clogged her throat, as even touching the rigid flesh caused her insides to seize up. She remembered what Bryston had looked like before the scar marred his chiseled face. But in truth, the disfigurement didn't detract from his rugged attraction.

Often, when she gazed upon him, she didn't even notice the disfigurement anymore.

His eyes grew hooded, and Bryston advanced until his thighs pressed into her. A jolt of excitement crackled through her, jarring, alarming, and tantalizing all at once.

"Lass, when ye look at me like that, yer gaze soft and yearnin', I vow I canna resist. Ye must ken there canna be anythin' between us."

And yet, despite his words, he cupped her chin with his long fingers, edging his mouth ever nearer to hers.

"Why no'?"

Why, ye numpty fool? Seriously?

Because he is still in love with his dead wife, that's why.

What mortal lass could compete with a woman raised to the status of sainthood in a man's memory? One he obviously idolized and worshipped.

Something akin to envy scratched away at her composure.

Branwen had always wished to fall in love and have a man cherish her with his whole heart, and if he were a man like Bryston McPherson?

Well, she'd count herself very blessed indeed.

"Because I canna offer what ye rightly deserve, Branwen. What every lass dreams of in the recesses of her heart."

His mouth was a scant hairsbreadth from hers.

If she but lifted her chin the merest bit...

"I canna give ye what yer heart longs for," he murmured, low and gruff and anguished.

Did he long for it as well?

Did memories and loyalty to Delphine ensnare him as surely as chains and shackles attached to a dank dungeon wall? He was a man tormented, and with everything in her, she ached to ease his suffering.

As she ran her gaze over his dear face, Branwen realized she was at a crossroads.

She could either take offense that he presumed to know what she wanted when they'd never spoken of this thing birthing between them, and thereby put him in his place and salvage her pride and dignity at his rejection.

Or, she could take a risk.

A monumental, possibly disastrous risk, and kiss him. Prove to him that perhaps he could move on with his life.

But what if he canna?

What if he can never care for another woman again?

Och, Branwen was already compromised as thoroughly as her beloved sister had been through no fault of her own. She might as well do something to earn her ruination. Unlike that, *this* she could control.

Standing on her tiptoes, she rested her palms against either side of Bryston's bristly face. "I think I ken what I need and want better than ye, Bryston McPherson, and I'll thank ye to nae be makin' decisions on my behalf."

Then she touched her mouth to his, and when he groaned low in his throat and crushed her to his hard chest, she promptly forgot entirely why she'd ever held any doubts as to whether she should or should not kiss him.

NINE

21 April 1721
Early Evening
Le Havre, France

Bryston patted the horse's wither as the friendly stable lad led the gelding into the mews behind the unexceptional, white-washed lodging house located in a respectable neighborhood several streets from Le Havre's harbor.

The sun hovered low on the bronze and berry-toned horizon, casting everything in a warm, golden glow as he hefted the bulging bag of garments for Branwen onto his shoulder. He'd placed the order yesterday morning and paid extra to have three gowns, a night rail, undergarments, stockings, a hairbrush and pins, a shawl, bonnet, and a few other feminine necessities ready by this afternoon.

It had rained earlier, and puddles dotted the ground here and there. A pair of songbirds bathed in a shallow pool until, sensing his perusal, they shook their wings and tails before flying away.

For the second day, he'd scoured Le Havre since after

breaking his fast at dawn, seeking information about Mical De La Beche. Delphine had once told him that her mother said her lover had hailed from Normandy. It only seemed logical to Bryston that, as a former pirate, De La Beche might be known in the area.

He'd been about to give up for the day when he'd encountered an old, stooped-shoulder sea salt at a seedy, smoke-filled pub on the waterfront. The shrunken man, deep wrinkles carved into his wizened face, claimed to have sailed with De La Beche over two decades ago.

After buying the nearly toothless tippler a bottle of superior rum and joining him in a dram, Bryston coaxed the information he'd sought from the sailor.

According to him, De La Beche was alive and well, and living in Rouen. On occasion, he ventured to Le Havre, but the former crew member hadn't seen him in a couple of years.

It seemed that shortly after leaving Tortuga all those years ago, Mical De La Beche had risen to the ranks of the respectable. He'd married a nobleman's daughter and now lived quite a luxurious life on a sprawling estate outside Rouen.

Bryston couldn't help but wonder if the pirate's change in status was the result of the mystical treasure.

Could it have really existed?

He scratched his jaw, then rolled his shoulders.

Mayhap.

Until now, he'd doubted its existence, mainly because Delphine had been so skeptical. But if so, De La Beche wouldn't be the first pirate to retire in comfort, living the remainder of his life off the wealth he'd acquired during his days of plundering and pillaging upon the high seas.

Bryston had spent the last hour making arrangements to hire a coach for the journey to Rouen on the morrow. He nodded at Jabir and Bayu sitting on a bench outside the inn as he approached.

Two yellow and white cats curled together near Jabir's feet, opened their citrine eyes, and watched his approach. Neither moved except for a single flick of the larger cat's white-tipped, striped tail. Evidently, determining Bryston wasn't a threat, they closed their eyes and resumed their naps.

"Any luck, Captain?" Bayu asked as he continued to sharpen one of his daggers after casting the bag a casual glance. "What have ye there?"

Bryston felt his neck heat. He didn't owe his men an explanation, and he certainly needn't feel chagrined for thinking of Branwen's comfort. "Och, just a few things for the lass. We fled so swiftly that she dinna have time to collect any of her belongin's."

"Quite so." Did Bayu's lips twitch the merest bit?

Jabir chuckled outright as he leaned down to scratch behind the purring cats' ears.

Insolent scunners.

Deciding that ignoring the clotheads was the wisest thing to do, Bryston placed his free hand on his hip. He glanced around, surveying the tidy circular drive and the potted plants on either side of the entrance. *Le Chien et le Coq,* The Hound and Cock, had been a good choice to stay at. Foreigners frequented the lodging house regularly, and Bryston didn't worry that he and the others would draw any unwanted attention.

"Aye," he said with a satisfied nod in answer to Bayu's first question. "De La Beche's in Rouen. Or at least he was."

"That is good news." Flashing a wide smile, Jabir nodded, his almost black eyes keen and alert. "All's quiet here, Captain. Your lady took a short walk earlier and is reading in the courtyard, just there."

He angled his big, shaven head toward a walled garden area a few feet away.

Branwen hadn't been happy about not being permitted to search for De La Beche with him. Still, after he'd explained precisely the types of establishments he meant to visit in his search for information, she'd reluctantly agreed.

He couldn't blame her for not wanting to see the inside of more brothels, particularly in France. She'd be thoroughly scandalized.

"I'll need four more men in addition to you and Jabir to travel with us as guards," he said to Bayu. "Let Zhao know, and tell him to send those most skilled at fighting. They need to be here at dawn. I intend to reach Rouen in less than two days."

There was no time to waste. Even now, Le Sauvage might be bearing down upon France. If he hadn't arrived before them. Not likely, but not impossible either.

"Aye, Captain," Bayu said, setting aside his honing stone before sliding his dagger into his waistband beside the other that rested there. He set off toward the wharf as Bryston headed toward the enclosed courtyard.

Branwen sat in one of four chairs situated beneath a wisteria-covered pergola. Thick clusters of purple flowers hung from the vine woven between the structure's braces. The sweet perfume hovered in the courtyard.

Eyes closed, she rested her ebony head against the chair's back, her open book lay spine up in her lap. No other guests occupied the quaint enclosed garden. No doubt they'd gone inside to eat their evening meal.

He allowed himself a few moments to study her, drinking in and memorizing each exquisite feature of this woman who intrigued him so.

Other than her dark hair, she was very different from Delphine.

Delphine's eyes had been an amber brown, her skin golden from the sun, and the top of her head didn't even reach his shoulder. She'd been quick to smile and laugh, and though she'd been a virgin when she came to their marriage bed, she hadn't been innocent or naive.

She couldn't read or write, but nonetheless possessed a worldly education Branwen would never know.

Branwen was taller, willowier, but no less alluring with lush, feminine curves he was honest enough to admit he itched to explore. Her gray eyes weren't cold, but they were assessing and shrewd.

More reserved than Delphine, she was formally educated but not as generous with her smiles. That wasn't to say Branwen didn't smile readily, but her countenance bore a thoughtful expression when at rest, while Delphine always seemed happy.

Delphine suffered from *mal de mer*. Branwen did not.

Branwen had a sister. Delphine was an only child.

Branwen had been fiercely protected and sheltered. Delphine had grown up unsupervised, running about the island, and exposed to all manner of unsavory situations.

Bryston had never felt the need to shield Delphine from the baseness of the world, but he didn't want Branwen exposed to such sordidness.

He shouldn't compare the two vastly different women: one raised on a tropical island amidst thieves, pirates, and scandalous women, and the other in the isolated wilds of Scotland, surrounded by a fiercely protective guardian and clansmen.

This compelling pull he felt toward Branwen Glanville didn't make sense.

She was nothing like Delphine, and yet his admiration for her bravery, stalwartness, and intrepidness grew daily.

Nae to mention her bonnie face and womanly assets.

Branwen hadn't complained once that she'd worn the same gown for over a week. Or that she'd been required to stay at the inn with little to do to occupy herself but read and take walks. Or that she missed her family. Nor had she railed at him in anger or accusation for stealing her away from Leith in such a high-handed manner and for exposing her to a whorehouse and prostitutes.

He'd specifically told her not to converse with the other guests at the inn lest word somehow leak out who she was and that she and Bryston were here. He had no way of knowing how far-reaching Le Sauvage's arm was. But the pirate *was* a Frenchman, and the French were unrepentantly loyal to their own.

Branwen stirred, a frown pleating her forehead before she settled again with a soft sigh. The movement drew his attention to her high, firm breasts. Not as bountiful as Delphine's, but more than enough to fill his palms. His mouth.

He scowled, noting her turned down mouth and the general air of despondency around her. Upon arrival at the inn, she'd asked at once if she might write to her family. Regretfully, he'd declined her request. Again, because he didn't know who to trust in this seaside community.

Bryston calculated Le Sauvage would find his way to France eventually. After all, he'd left a few crumbs along the way to lead the blackguard here. Branwen thought Le Sauvage voyaged to the Caribbean, and that was what Bryston wanted her to think.

He wouldn't have her looking over her shoulder or starting at every unknown sound. That was why he'd assigned men to watch her, to bring her a degree of peace.

Zhao had told him, once they'd made the open sea, that he'd sabotaged Le Sauvage's ship, thereby preventing the scapegrace from immediately following *The Dolphin*. He'd also *accidentally* spread the word that *The Dolphin* sailed to Port de Lyon rather than Le Havre.

Bryston intended to lure Marc-André Le Sauvage into a trap and then finish the bastard off. He'd tortured and killed Delphine, and every minute the devil's spawn remained breathing was a crime against justice and humanity.

Branwen knew nothing of this scheme. Bryston had meant to tell her when the time was right, but he also didn't want her fretting unnecessarily.

After they reached Rouen.

Aye, that was when he'd tell her.

Unable to resist, Bryston crossed to Branwen and knelt on one knee before her chair, setting the satchel down too. She'd braided her glorious hair, and the thick rope trailed over her left shoulder and nestled between her breasts.

Lucky thing.

"Branwen?" He touched her hand, not wanting to startle her.

Her sooty lashes fluttered, and she opened drowsy, disoriented quicksilver eyes. For several heartbeats, she gazed at Bryston unguarded and her soft mouth curved sweetly as she looked at him with unrestrained and undisguised affection.

He bent his mouth into a wistful smile, wishing with his entire being that he could give her what he so clearly saw she desired.

Until Le Sauvage was dead, he couldn't contemplate a different future than what he'd decided upon when Delphine had died.

But that was before Branwen needed ye. Before Le Sauvage

rose from the dead. Ye can carve a new future for yerself, an inner voice whispered.

Could he?

The veriest infinitesimal spark of hope ignited.

Nothing more than an ember, weak and pitiful and easily snuffed. But it was a beginning—more than he'd believed ever possible again.

Then, as if reading something in his expression, Branwen blinked, her lashes feathering across her alabaster cheeks. Whatever affection or sentiment had reflected in her eyes the second before was replaced by inquisitiveness when she raised them to his again.

She sat up, closing her book and setting it aside. She flung her braid behind her back and smoothed her slate-blue gown's deeply creased skirts. Her expression expectant, she asked, "Did ye discover anythin'?"

Standing, he gazed around to make sure they were alone and that no errant ears listened in on their conversation.

"Aye," he said low. "We leave for Rouen at dawn on the morrow."

Her eyes went round, and she skimmed a cursory glance about the courtyard before licking her lower lip. She rose and stepped near to Bryston. Instead of the heather and lavender fragrance he'd become accustomed to, he caught a whiff of lemon and rose.

The soap she'd used to bathe with these past two days.

Ridiculous as it was, Bryston grieved the loss of *her* scent.

"Is *he* there?" she asked, scarcely above a whisper. "Ye're takin' me with ye?"

Bryston didn't need to ask who *he* was.

He dipped his chin in affirmation. How could she think he'd leave her behind? "Aye, and six of my best fighters will accompany us."

Her eyes glittered with satisfaction and a hint of that emotion she tried so valiantly to hide from him. "Are ye pleased to have found him? I ken this must be verra hard for ye."

"Aye, I am."

Not once, not one single time, had she voiced concern for herself.

The truth of her situation lay as an unspoken complication between them.

After she'd kissed him two days ago, the ship, his crew, and the very ocean itself had disappeared until there was only Branwen in his arms. Branwen's oh so delicious, velvety soft mouth beneath his. Branwen pressing herself against him and making the most erotic little noises in her throat.

He'd known. Known beyond a doubt that he felt something for Branwen, the brave, proud lass. And she unabashedly felt something for him too.

And God help him, he wanted to kiss her again. Wanted to do a whole lot more with Branwen Glanville, truth to tell. Wished to lay her across a bed in broad daylight and trail his mouth over every naked inch of her.

Christ.

As if reading his erotic thoughts, she stepped nearer and placed one hand upon his chest. Her face upturned, a question in the depths of those spectacular eyes, she lashed into his reverie.

Do ye want me? Branwen's stunning silvery eyes silently entreated.

Aye.

Aye, leannán, I do. Odin's bones, I do.

If Bryston didn't kiss her, taste her mouth, mingling his breath with hers, he'd go mad. He cupped her face, and a ragged sigh escaped her as their lips met.

Fool, he chided. *This can never be.*

Mayhap, his heart countered. *Mayhap it can, once Le Sauvage is dealt with.*

Branwen parted her mouth, and he slipped his tongue inside, parrying and jousting with hers. He clasped her around her trim waist, needing her closer and yet closer still.

A small mewling moan escaped her, and she plunged her fingers into the hair at the back of his head, holding him to her hungry mouth.

A coarse laugh echoed from inside the inn, followed by the sound of glass breaking, then an outraged, haughty male diatribe in rapid French.

Bryston eased away, reluctantly withdrawing his mouth from hers.

"Bryston?" she whispered, uncertain and confused, the warmth of her breath wisping against his open mouth. His breath came in short pants, a raging erection pulsing at his groin.

"Och, Branwen. I ken."

And he did know, finding it as impossible as she to put into words whatever this was enthralling them both. He rested his forehead against hers while trailing a finger over her creamy cheek with his forefinger.

"Now isna the time, Branwen. We'll discuss it later, I vow to ye."

After this business with De La Beche and Le Sauvage had been dealt with.

She shifted away, stumbling over the bag he'd left by her chair.

He caught her elbow and steadied her.

Glancing down, she eyed the overstuffed satchel. "What is that?"

She brought her gaze up to meet his.

"A few things I picked up for ye. Gowns, gloves, and the like." Items she'd never have asked him for, he'd learned.

"Thank ye. That was verra thoughtful of ye." Her expression softened, her gaze seeking his as gratitude made her beautiful face glow.

God's teeth.

When she looked at him that way, Bryston believed anything was possible.

Hadn't the king recently awarded him The Most Ancient and Most Noble Order of the Thistle, and also bestowed estates upon him for capturing and bringing to justice those conspiring against His Majesty?

Bryston was respectable now, and wealthy too.

Respectable enough for a woman like Branwen?

He'd never cared about respectability with Delphine, and self-recrimination and hot betrayal roiled in his gut.

"Shall we dine, lass?"

"Do I have time to change?" she asked huskily, her lips red and swollen from his ravenous kisses.

Was she embarrassed to wear the same gown a third night in the dining room?

"Aye." He nodded and swallowed.

He wasn't the least hungry for food. Nae, what he wanted was the luscious woman before him. But could he break a vow he'd made to his dead wife?

Wouldn't that make him the worst sort of disloyal bastard?

He greatly feared that the silver-eyed beauty had bewitched him already, and it was too late for doubts and recriminations.

I'm sorry, Delphine.
Forgive me, my sweet tropical flower.
I've failed ye, the treasure of my heart.

TEN

24 April 1721
Hôtel De La Rouen
Rouen, France

Standing at the tall window of her chamber in the *Hôtel De La Rouen*, overlooking a bustling city street, Branwen awaited Bryston. She wasn't nervous precisely, but neither was she at ease.

Resolving to calm her nerves and to force the wings fluttering about her belly to settle, she placed her palms to her midriff and inhaled slowly and deliberately to the count of five, then counted to five once more as she released the deep breath.

Better.

Not much, but she welcomed the reprieve, small though it was.

She glanced down at her hands, still pressed against her middle.

Of the three gowns Bryston had purchased for her, this was the finest—a rich sherry red-colored wool with a delicate lace collar and sleeves. A maid had twisted her hair into a simple chignon, leaving two long curls to trail over her right shoulder. She wore the same simple pearl earrings she'd been wearing that day at Holyrood Abbey.

Never in her wildest conjectures could she have anticipated what the last several days had brought her. That sense of discontent had diffused as Bryston had plunged her headlong into a misadventure of monumental proportions.

Brushing her fingertips across the fine, soft cloth, Branwen quirked her mouth into a rueful smile. She mightn't be attired appropriately for a High Society assembly in Edinburgh, but no fault could be found in the gown's simple elegance. Her scuffed shoes, on the other hand...

Pshaw.

Wrinkling her nose, she scanned the damp street for the umpteenth time, quite fascinated with some of the French fashions she'd seen. In truth, she didn't much care whether Mical De La Beche or his lady found her appearance wanting.

Aye, she was the ward of a powerful Scottish duke, but only the opinion of one man mattered to her.

She touched her fingertip to the cool glass, a small smile playing around the edges of her mouth. Rivulets of rain made irregular paths down the pane, and horses' hooves splashed muddy water in their wake on the lane below.

Something had occurred after sharing that wondrous kiss with Bryston three days ago. An unspoken agreement that they'd wait until these matters with Le Sauvage and De La Beche were settled, and then they'd examine this compelling, undeniable attraction between them.

At least she thought that was what Bryston had meant when he'd said not now.

"Now isna the time, Branwen. We'll discuss it later, I vow to ye."

If she weren't mistaken—and she didn't believe she was—he'd been as overtaken with emotion and passion as she had been.

Did that mean he was ready to move on at last?

That he could put his wife's death behind him?

Honestly, Branwen didn't know, nor could she allow herself to ruminate on that very critical point. She'd simply have to wait as Bryston had asked. If she'd been prudent, she'd have bargained with him, agreed to wait, but only after extracting a promise the situation wouldn't be ignored or brushed under a rug indefinitely.

She breathed out a lengthy sigh, her shoulders slumping the merest bit.

Dinna sulk, she scolded herself. *Or think the worst.*

Well, in a few hours, at least they'd know one way or the other about the mysterious treasure that had caused so much trouble. Och, it wasn't gold or jewels that caused the problems, but greedy men.

How many times throughout history had that been the case?

Untold times.

Bryston had located De La Beche's home yesterday, and they would call upon the former pirate this afternoon. Her tummy tightened in anticipation.

Their journey to Rouen had been tediously uneventful. Boring, even. Only intermittent rain showers, three hares tearing across the road and startling the team, and becoming stuck in the mud once had broken the monotony of the trip.

Bryston had ridden inside the coach, causing the interior to shrink with his hulking presence, while his six dangerous-looking crew members had acted as reluctant outriders. Amongst the items he'd procured for her was a small silver-handled dagger.

"In case ye need to defend yerself," he'd said a trifle too casually.

Keane had taught her and Bethea how to wield a dirk for self-protection, but she'd never used a weapon this small and wasn't positive how effective the five-inch blade might be against even an average-sized man.

Unaccustomed to the long hours in the saddle, more than one of his crew had groused about their sore rumps when they stopped. "I'll take the rollin' deck of a ship any day over the boney back of a horse," Scags had declared while rubbing that part of his person paining him before discreetly taking a swig from the flask he'd slid from his pocket.

Branwen had hidden a smile behind her hand.

The man had no extra flesh upon him anywhere, and it was no wonder his posterior ached. That he was one of Bryston's most skilled fighters came as a surprise since he didn't look strong enough to lift a butter knife, let alone a sword.

Tap. Tap-tap-tap. Tap.

Ah, Bryston's signal.

Her heartbeat accelerated in anticipation, waiting for him to repeat the knock as they'd discussed.

Did he truly expect Le Sauvage to appear and spirit her away?

The thought made her cringe inwardly, and a shudder rippled across her shoulders.

On the two-day journey to Rouen, he revealed that Le Sauvage most likely hadn't sailed to the tropics but was, instead, hot on their trail. That caused her no small amount of discomfiture. Yet she wholeheartedly trusted Bryston to know how to deal with the pirate.

After all, he'd been a buccaneer himself.

He would be quick to correct her and remind her he'd

been a privateer—vast difference from a common pirate or swashbuckler—at the behest of His Majesty himself. Unlike Le Sauvage and many other pillagers of the sea, Bryston possessed an honorable heart and abided by a strict code of ethics.

She furrowed her forehead while running the fingers of one hand down the length of the deep green drapery festooning the leaded glass window.

In truth, she suspected Le Sauvage would never leave off his mad pursuit, even when faced with an irrefutable truth that no treasure existed. Or, if it ever had, De La Beche had retrieved it himself, which accounted for his wealth, as Bryston believed was the case.

What would Le Sauvage do then?

Would he be content to leave them be?

In truth, she also worried Bryston wouldn't be satisfied, wouldn't ever be completely at peace, as long as his wife's murderer roamed free.

Her heart flipped over as it did whenever she thought of Delphine's death and Bryston's grief. He felt something for Branwen, she knew it to be true. But was the sentiment as strong and compelling as what burned behind her ribcage for him?

An emotion that grew daily, an unrelenting burgeoning that consumed her thoughts?

Could Bryston ever care for another with the intensity he had loved his wife?

Was it fair to expect that from him?

She wasn't sure what she believed about soulmates and some people only being able to love one person their entire lives. Even crows, rooks, and ravens found a new mate when theirs died.

But what if Bryston couldn't?

Could Branwen be content as second-best if he would have her?

Would she grow tired of trying to please him and win his affection?

Was this feeling engulfing her powerful enough to persevere for years, despite knowing she'd never be loved, cherished, or adored, as she'd longed for since girlhood?

Biting her lower lip, she shook her head.

She just didn't know.

Which was worse?

To love someone and let them go because they couldn't ever love you? Or to try to make a life with them, knowing their heart would always belong to someone else?

Yer gettin' ahead of yerself Branwen Tara Patience Glanville. He's made nae declaration, and neither has he spoken of a future together, let alone marriage.

She inhaled another lengthy, cleansing breath.

One thing at a time.

First things first: De La Beche. Le Sauvage. Then she and Bryston.

Tap. Tap-tap-tap. Tap.

Bryston knocked again.

"Comin'," she called as she hurried across the scratched but clean wood floor to unlock the door.

He'd insisted it remain locked whenever she was in the chamber.

After opening the door, she stood aside for him to enter. He gave her one of his cocky grins as he took in her gown and hair. When he looked at her like that, smoldering interest in his eyes, she couldn't help but believe he cared for her.

"Lass, ye are a vision. Ye put God's glorious sunrises and sunsets to shame, ye do." He winked and puffed out his chest in an exaggerated manner. "I shall be the envy of every man in

France." He shook his head, that blond mane of his brushing his shoulders. "Nae, all of Europe." He spread his arms wide. "The *world*."

She wrinkled her nose at his obvious silly antics to put her at ease as she closed the door behind him. "Ye'd say that to anythin' I wore as long as it wasna that creased and stained travesty I wore for over a week straight."

In truth, she was heartily sick of that gown herself.

"Nae, ye ken that isna true." His expression turned somber, and that light shone in his deep brown eyes that sent her pulse capering and the rest of her heating like a kettle simmering over an open fire. "Ye could wear rags, lass, and I'd think ye utterly exquisite."

A flush of pleasure made her cheeks prickle with warmth. She grinned and, hands on her hips, tossed her head. "That's because my namesake was the daughter of the mythical King Llyr. Did ye ken she's the Welsh goddess of love and beauty?"

"Och, ye dinna say?" He eyed her speculatively, a merry twinkle in his eyes. "Love *and* beauty? Disna seem fair to the other goddesses that ye should have two."

This flirting with him was fun, neither of them daring to say yet what simmered in their hearts.

Please, God and all the divine powers. Dinna let me be mistaken about his feelin's for me.

Bryston glanced around her chamber, taking in the neatly made bed, her other garments hanging from pegs on the wall, and the open window to let the fresh air in.

"Are ye ready?" he asked.

He wore a fine woolen dark blue jacket and matching waistcoat today. The same clothing he'd worn at the Earl of Montieth's ball, if she weren't mistaken. Though undeniably striking in the fancy attire, she preferred the ship's captain in his usual long leather doublet. That was the Bryston

McPherson she'd come to know and love these past several days.

Her breath stuttered to a halt, and she dropped her focus to his boots lest he see the shocked realization that surely shone in her eyes.

She loved him.

How could that be true?

Shouldn't it take weeks, even months, to fall in love?

Nae, Marjorie and Keane had fallen in love almost at first sight. In fact, she could count on two hands a number of Keane's Highlander friends who'd lost their hearts to worthy women in a very short amount of time.

Once given, the heart of a Scot was faithful, loyal, and enduring.

"Branwen?" He gave her a quizzical look as she raised her eyes to his, afraid he'd see the truth reflected there.

"Aye, just let me collect my cloak," she said, fashioning a benign smile.

Before she could retrieve the garment from the hook near the door, he'd removed it and held it open for her.

With a small, appreciative nod, she turned her back and nearly sighed with contentment when he wrapped it around her shoulders. But instead of stepping away, he drew her against the broad, hard planes of his chest and pressed his lips to her hair.

"Dinna fash yerself, nae matter what happens today, Branwen."

His masculine scent surrounded her, and she closed her eyes for a blink, absorbing him. The feeling of his muscular arms encircling her made her feel safe. The wonder of his manly contours pressed into her softer form.

This man. This inscrutable, complex man. Spy.

Highlander. Buccaneer. Fierce and kind. Powerful warrior and gentle giant. Lord, how she loved him.

She turned her head to gaze into his seductive eyes. Eyes, she wanted to sink into. To see upon wakening first thing every morning as the sun rose.

As it often did of late, her wretched attention dipped to his mouth.

How could a man's mouth be so bloody tempting?

Nae, no' any mon's mouth. Bryston's.

His lips curved minutely at her avid inspection, and she hadn't a doubt he, too, remembered the blistering kiss they'd exchanged.

Bending his neck, he whispered near her cheek, sending a rush of awareness crackling through her. Never had she been so in tune with another person, not even her sister.

"In good time, lass. In good time. Ye ken?"

Another promise?

What, exactly, did he mean by that?

Branwen opened her mouth to ask when urgent pounding rattled the door. As one, she and Bryston turned toward the entry.

His brows lashed together as he wrapped his fingers around the handle of his dirk.

At once, she slipped her hand into the pocket of her gown. Curling her palm around the cold, hard metal, she awaited Bryston's cue.

"Captain? Are ye in there?" Bayu spoke low and intense.

In three lumbering strides, Bryston was at the door, yanking it open.

His expression grim, Bayu glanced past Bryston to Branwen, then swung his attention back. "Jabir spied two of Le Sauvage's dogs not more than a half-hour ago."

ELEVEN

Later that afternoon
Outside Rouen, France

Bryston swore a litany of vulgar curses inwardly during the forty-five-minute drive to De La Beche's estate. He'd thought to have time to interview De La Beche and warn him about Le Sauvage before the bastard tracked them to Rouen.

He wasn't concerned for himself. After all, he knew how to fight, but there was De La Beche's wife and possibly his children to consider if he had any, as well as Branwen's safety and his men's, of course.

Le Sauvage hadn't acquired his name by being merciful or compassionate.

Bryston's crew's willingness to help him capture Delphine's murderer, no matter how dangerous the task, further touched that previously dead place inside him that Branwen had awakened. It made Bryston wonder if he mightn't take to the sea again after all.

From beneath half-lowered lids, he observed her and the play of muted light flickering across her smooth cheeks as the carriage jostled along. She'd taken to sea like a mermaid, and he didn't doubt she'd enjoy venturing to new lands as well.

Hadn't her father been a sea captain?

Aye. Bryston strongly suspected the sea was in the lass's blood too.

He'd observed it in the way she lifted her face to the spray, the private smile tickling the edges of her lush mouth as she watched the dolphins and the waves, in the way she closed her eyes and breathed in the salty air.

They'd make a good pair, they would.

As if sensing he watched her, she flicked a swift look at him before darting her pale gray gaze away. Her expression was indiscernible, but he knew questions bubbled beneath that calm mien.

Did he care for her?

Could they have a future together?

Could they be happy?

Could he ever truly put what happened to his wife behind him?

Did he want to?

Honestly, he didn't have exact answers for some of those unspoken questions, but he did admit to a strong inclination for others.

He pointedly turned his musings to what was to transpire in a few short minutes.

De La Beche knew Bryston was calling today, but all he'd told him was that it had something to do with concern for his safety. He hadn't decided yet whether to tell the man he was Delphine's father.

Bryston pressed a knuckle into his temple, something he often did when deep in thought.

The truth of it was, this meeting with De La Beche was likely a waste of time, but he'd been at a loss as to how to lure

Le Sauvage into a trap. He wasn't even certain he'd face punishment in France for killing Delphine, though Tortuga was a French colony.

He'd witnesses aplenty who could attest to the murder besides himself.

Even if Le Sauvage heard from De La Beche's mouth himself that there was no treasure buried on a tropical island or hidden in a secret cave along some craggy Atlantic coastline, Le Sauvage was mad enough to not believe him.

The question still niggled as to where Le Sauvage had been these past five years?

There'd not been a single sighting of the man.

No whispers or rumors.

Nothing after his ship supposedly foundered in a hurricane in the Atlantic after he'd killed Delphine and fled Tortuga.

"Bryston? Are ye all right?"

He'd been clenching his jaw so hard that he'd ground his teeth together.

Branwen had watched him keenly on and off since he'd bundled her into the conveyance, along with extra loaded blunderbusses. His men were equally equipped with weapons.

Jabir drove the rented equipage, Bayu and Scags riding atop with weapons at the ready. Two of the other guards flanked the vehicle, and the third rode a few feet behind. Now he wished he'd asked more men to accompany them.

All of his crew wore garments appropriate for French commoners, but no one who took one look at Jabir or Bayu would mistake them for such.

Especially not Le Sauvage.

"Bryston?" she said his name again, leaning forward to place her palm upon his knee.

Sensation sluiced up his thigh, straight to his groin, which grew heavy with need.

It wasn't any wonder.

He hadn't bedded a woman since Delphine's death, and for days now, he'd imagined joining with Branwen to the point he'd awoken several nights with a marble-hard cockstand. Aye, he'd relieved himself with his hand while envisioning the raven-haired beauty, and imagining her glorious body unclothed and writhing beneath his.

It was either tend to the task himself or risk perpetual embarrassment and heckling by his men for his obvious arousal and desire for the lass.

France was known for its many erotic houses of pleasure, the likes of which were touted all over the world, yet he couldn't bring himself to bed a prostitute, no matter how skilled she might be in the art of pleasing a man.

Not when he only wanted one woman, and she sat across from him, poised and serene.

He covered her hand with his own. "Aye, I'm just thinkin', *leannán.*"

Her mouth and eyes softened with his endearment, but she didn't ask about what. Nonetheless, the question lingered in her eyes.

He knew her though.

She wouldn't pry, no matter how curious she might be.

He appreciated that about Branwen. She allowed him the space he needed to work things out in his mind. And also with his emotions, which, at present, were a maelstrom of confusion and vexation and, aye, lust.

Even now, desire hummed through him.

He'd seen the yearning in her gorgeous eyes, tasted it in her unskilled but passionate kisses. Aye, this lass had wiggled her way past his barricades and managed to worm her way into a heart he'd believed too mangled to ever feel anything again.

But Bryston did feel something for her.

Something incredibly compelling.

Different than what he'd experienced with Delphine, but no less meaningful or forceful in its intensity. Just *different.* He couldn't think of another word to accurately describe it. And how could the sentiment not be different? They were two vastly diverse women, each unique and marvelous.

But was it love?

Could he permit himself to love another woman and betray his promise to Delphine?

Couldn't he hold Branwen in deep affection, respect and admire her, and most definitely lust after her delectable body? Weren't many marriages built on far less?

Giving him a winsome closed-mouth smile, Branwen turned her attention to the passing countryside.

For certain, she must harbor fear and trepidation, yet she'd remained ever stoic and undaunted. Her trust in Bryston humbled him. And, Odin's teeth, filled him with absolute terror.

Another had trusted him absolutely as well, and he'd failed her. He'd left her alone while he sought Le Sauvage, only to find the cur had slithered into his home and destroyed that which was most precious to him.

By damn, he wouldn't leave Branwen in a strange hotel in a foreign land and risk that horror happening all over again. True, she didn't know anything about the treasure, but that didn't mean La Sauvage wouldn't exploit her to manipulate Bryston.

Tapping the fingers of one hand on his thigh, he considered his choice to take her with him. How many times over these past several days had he wondered if Keane would've been able to protect her and his family?

Doubted himself for dragging her along?

The truth was, nothing in life was certain or absolute. No decision he made was absolutely right or wrong. There were too many uncontrollable variables. At the time, it seemed the most prudent thing to do. Because some churl had planted a maggot in Le Sauvage's head that Branwen was Bryston's woman.

Isna she?

Aye, mayhap now, even though he hadn't declared himself, but she wasn't mere days ago.

And underlying all of his pondering and plotting was a burning question. Why had Le Sauvage come after him again?

In Leith, bringing Branwen with him had seemed logical, but he hadn't expected the attraction he'd felt for her to explode into consuming emotion. However, he could not dwell on that at present. He must concentrate all of his efforts and focus on destroying Le Sauvage, or he'd never find peace. And he risked making a mistake or becoming careless.

More on point, Branwen would never be safe as long as Le Sauvage roamed free.

His heart swelled with emotion. He might not be able to vow undying love, but he didn't want to lose this lass. She meant something to him, and if marrying her was how he could guarantee she'd be a part of his life, he could do that and still be faithful to his dead wife's memory.

He could marry Branwen, hold her in deep regard, perhaps have children in time, and still be faithful to Delphine's memory if he didn't permit himself to love her.

Bryston didn't deserve Branwen, but if she'd have him, he'd make her his wife. For she alone had been able to ease the torment in his soul and bring a degree of contentment to him that he never thought to know again.

He was a bloody, selfish bastard.

Aye, he was.

An unmitigated, hell-fired arse.

Nonetheless, he'd ask her to be his wife, and she could choose where they lived. Even take to the sea with him, if that was what she desired.

He ought to wait until the matter with Le Sauvage was settled, but if he could persuade her, he'd like to wed before they left France.

A derisive snort almost escaped him.

Hadn't he vowed to himself mere days ago that he'd do no such thing?

Aye, but he hadn't spent days in her company then either, hadn't realized how perfect she was for him, hadn't known the transformation to his soul she'd cause.

"Branwen?" He scooted to the opposite seat to sit beside her and took her delicate, gloved hand in his. "Lass, we'll arrive shortly, and before we do, there's somethin' important I'd say to ye."

He kissed the back of her wrist where her pulse thrummed along at a speedy clip.

"Aye?" Eyes shining, brimming with unfettered hope, she tightly clasped his hand.

Chuckling, he chucked her under her pert chin. "There's nothin' subtle about ye, lass."

"Ye'd have me dissemble and feign indifference?" A frown crinkled her forehead, and she pursed those plump red pillows of her mouth. "Ye ken me better than that, Bryston McPherson. I've always been straightforward with ye, and ye with me. 'Tis why we get along as well as we do."

"Aye, I do ken ye."

With a little sniff, she angled her chin. "Well? Did ye wish to say somethin' or no'?"

Hadn't he just been thinking she wasn't the prying sort?

Aye, she'd not pry, but she'd prod—ruthlessly.

"Indeed." He grinned, delighted at her ruffled feathers and the two bright spots on her cheeks. He drew her soft curves into the circle of his arms. "I would like ye to consider an offer."

A fine midnight eyebrow quirked, but she remained silent even as she melted further into his embrace.

God, she was so womanly soft, and she smelled divine.

His cock jerked to attention.

"As ye ken, the king bequeathed me estates and a fancily worded award of some sort. I am a man of means, though humbly born. I love the sea, but as ye ken, I am capable of givin' her up. I completed my last mission for His Majesty as an agent, which makes me a free man to do as I wish now."

He gazed into her eyes, willing her to understand how difficult it was for him to say more.

"And yer tellin' me this *because*?"

The vixen wasn't going to make this easy on him.

"Ye ken, I said we'd have a discussion later."

She nodded. "Ye did after ye kissed me."

"Ye kissed me too, lass." Even to his own ears, his voice sounded raspy with unchecked desire.

Her attention lowered to his mouth, and her lips parted. "Aye, I did," she replied huskily.

She cleared her throat, then wet her lips.

Bloody hell. How much torment could a man take?

"What, exactly, are ye tryin' to say, Bryston?"

He braced himself and then dove in like a man jumping from a craggy cliff into the foaming sea below.

"Branwen, if ye'll have me, I'd take ye as my wife. I ken we could be happy together either livin' on one of my estates or sailin' the world pickin' up and deliverin' cargo. Or..." He hesitated, trying to determine what she'd want. "Even livin' near yer sister or Edinburgh if that is what ye prefer."

Anywhere, as long as we can be together.

She'd become his lifeline, his connection to a happier future. And God, how he wanted to numb the pain eviscerating him every hour of every day. Nae, not numb the pain, but rid himself of it. And for the first time, he was optimistic that was a possibility.

Her eyes became silver pools of emotion as she cupped his cheek with her palm, staring intently into his eyes, as if seeking to touch his very soul.

And she did touch it.

He felt the melding, the joining, much like an iron and carbonite alloy to create sturdy, strong, and enduring steel.

"Bryston, do ye love me?"

The words were so softly uttered that he barely heard them, and he knew what courage it had taken her to ask the question. The risk of humiliation and rejection. The craving in her spirit to know that simple truth.

A truth she had every right to.

Marshaling his courage to tell her, he slanted his focus away for a fraction—no more than a heartbeat, in truth—but it was enough for her to stiffen and then gently extract herself from his embrace.

Dammit.

"Ye dinna." Her soft murmur lanced his conscience.

It wasn't an accusation. Nevertheless, hurt fairly dripped from the two short words. Chin high and shoulders back, majestic and proud, Branwen wrapped her cloak tighter around herself as if trying to buffer herself from further pain.

Also, as if trying to convince him that he hadn't cleaved

her in two, though he'd never intentionally harm her in any way.

His gut wrenched sickeningly, and Bryston cursed himself for speaking too soon. He was a selfish bastard, wanting to tie her to him because she'd made him feel alive again. Yet he couldn't vow the one thing—three little life-altering words— she most needed to hear him say.

Not yet, in any event.

In truth, likely not ever.

He couldn't permit it.

Loyalty and devotion to another couldn't be dismissed so summarily.

"I understand." She presented her profile, but not before he saw the sheen of tears in her now pewter-gray eyes. "What ye had with Delphine was special. A once in a lifetime emotion. She was yer soulmate."

"Branwen." He touched her upper arm, but she jerked away as if burned by a blazing hot blade.

Only moments before, she'd cuddled into him, and now she sat rigid and radiating mortification and pain.

"Lass, I feel somethin powerful for ye. No' what I felt for my wife, but 'tis deep and abidin'. I canna say for certain if 'tis love, even though I ken that is what ye wish me to tell ye. I ken ye'd have honesty between us."

"Why propose then?"

Because I need ye. I dinna understand it.

She cocked her head, looking quite adorably like an inquisitive bird.

"Did ye think I'd jump at the chance to save my reputation? Or is it to escape Keane's wrath, for we both ken he'll be livid with ye. Or do ye simply want my body, and yer too honorable to satiate yer lust without exchangin' vows first?" She skimmed a scornful gaze over him. "Nae, likely the latter when ye know the madam of a whorehouse on a given name basis."

Anger tempered each snapped word, and he didn't blame her—couldn't summon a morsel of offense.

However, waiting to ask her to be his wife wouldn't have changed the facts.

A sigh filled with a torrent of regret and resignation whooshed from Bryston as he pushed away from her and maneuvered to the other side of the carriage once more. "Forgive me for speakin' out of turn. I had nae right to ask ye."

She didn't respond but huddled further into her corner. "When do I return home?"

Well, he had his answer.

Why, then, did it feel like he'd been keelhauled? Flogged with a cat o' nine tails?

"As soon as I ken for certain that Le Sauvage isna a threat to ye, lass."

Possibly, she was safer with Keane at Trentwick now. Especially now that the spy who'd infiltrated the castle had rejoined Le Sauvage.

She folded her arms and elevated an eyebrow. "Och, then it seems to me, the wisest thing to do if ye want the cur captured and prosecuted for Delphine's death is to let him think we *are* married. Willna he come after me to get to ye? Then ye can be done with the scunner, once and for all, and I can go home."

Nae lass, I dinna want to lose ye.

Too late, his heart cried, mourning the loss already.

TWELVE

Châteaux de Beaumont
Outside Rouen, France

Thirty minutes later, Branwen and Bryston awaited their hosts in quite the most elaborately appointed drawing room she'd ever seen. The French were known for their opulent taste in décor, and this room with its gilded portraits, plaster moldings, and, in general, wholly overdone architecture left her quite stunned.

Still reeling with humiliation and fulminating compunction, her heart ached painfully. Each breath was a supreme effort. Nonetheless, she affected nonchalance as she studied the room, keeping her back to Bryston as much as possible.

She felt his brooding gaze on her as sure as if he'd placed a hand upon her rigid spine. He watched her every movement.

Had it only been mere hours ago when Branwen had wondered if she could make a happy, contented life with someone she knew didn't love her?

Had she truly naively believed *her* love would be enough?

The instant Branwen had asked Bryston if he loved her,

she could've bitten off her tongue. She'd forced his hand, but now she was glad for her impulsiveness. An undeniable truth had reared its head during those extended, awkward moments in the carriage.

She *could not* be contented with a man who didn't love her, no matter how much she loved him.

Fool. Numpty. Imbecile.

Branwen had been deluding herself.

Just as well she know the truth of it now, rather than continue to harbor false hope. That someday he might come to love her. Branwen wasn't a wagering woman, and that gamble was far too risky to take.

Nevertheless, she respected Bryston for his honesty.

He could've easily lied to get what he wanted. To seduce her into his bed.

Oh, she hadn't a doubt he wanted her body, but he craved carnal satisfaction and nothing more. And once they'd wed and she learned the heartbreaking truth, it would've destroyed her.

As it was now, her heart and pride were battered—*fine, pulverized*—but she still had her dignity. Gone were the foolish, false illusions she'd entertained these past several days.

How well could one get to know another in less than a fortnight, anyway?

Well enough to know there will never be another like Bryston McPherson.

That comprehension effectively and immediately dissolved any lingering anger.

How could she fault Bryston for feeling the same way about Delphine that Branwen felt for him?

The heart was an intrepid thing, and it loved whom it loved.

There was no place for blame, accusation, resentment, regrets, or even logic.

Branwen resisted the urge to glance over her shoulder to see what Bryston was doing.

He hadn't spoken more than a dozen words to her since they'd disembarked the carriage. Once he'd given his men their orders, he'd escorted her inside the mansion, all cool formality and politesse.

Craning her neck, Branwen gawked unabashedly at the ornamentation, the garish plum and gold furnishings, the bright marble-topped tables, and the vases of flowers on nearly every surface. Gold-framed mirrors, candelabras, and chandeliers reflected the ribbons of sunlight streaming in from the six floor-to-ceiling windows gracing one side of the room.

Between every two windows, French windows opened up onto a raised terrace, upon which a gardener had artfully arranged planters, benches, and statues. Beyond the terrace lay breathtaking gardens, the likes of which she'd never before seen.

If a single spent blossom or stray leaf marred even one meticulously tended bed, she'd flip her skirts up as Abbie and her girls had upon the docks.

Either Mical De La Beche had married very well, or he had indeed acquired a vast fortune from his pirating days. Nonetheless, as remarkable as the house was, she could not imagine living in such a place.

Aye, it might be beautiful and ostentatious, but it lacked any warmth, and she would never be able to relax in such elegant surroundings.

Meandering across the glossy, dark nut-hued parquet floor, she inspected a portrait of a slender, distinguished gentleman with a roguish sparkle in his eyes.

He stood behind the chair of a plump, petite dark-haired

woman, not particularly pretty but regal and with an unmistakable air of confidence. Surrounding them were six lads of varying ages, and a chubby infant girl swathed in white lace reclined upon her mother's lap.

"Do ye think that's him?" She angled her head toward the painting.

Bryston joined her, scar standing out in stark contrast against his sun-browned skin. "I dinna ken."

"'Tis magnificent, *non*?"

They turned as one to see the object of the portrait stride into the room.

Perhaps in his middling fifties, De La Beche wore a broad grin as he swept an affectionate glance over the painting. He pointed at the artwork with his unpretentious, curved silver-handled walking cane. "'Twas painted eight years ago. Alas, all my *les enfants* except my daughter are at school, and my wife took her to visit her family today."

Attired in an unadorned burgundy suit and a gold-trimmed silk, ivory doublet, he bespoke understated elegance. He wore a simple chestnut brown wig, black-buckled shoes, and a single ring set with a sapphire glinted on the forefinger of his left hand.

Though he sported a tidily trimmed beard, Mical De La Beche wasn't at all what she'd expected in a former pirate captain. Though, of course, she'd only ever known Bryston and seen Le Sauvage the one time. Of average height, nothing in De La Beche's attire, bearing, or expression hinted at his former scandalous life.

He turned a penetrating gaze upon Bryston.

Except *that* look.

That unequivocally was a captain's unflinching, expectant perusal.

"I suggested such a visit to my wife's sister might be

prudent after receiving your brusque message, Captain McPherson, *non?*"

"Wise of ye, De La Beche," Bryston said. He indicated Branwen with a sweep of his hand. "Permit me to introduce Branwen Glanville, ward of the Duke of Roxdale of Trentwick Castle."

He didn't bother with a formal introduction, which didn't surprise her. Nor did he explain why Branwen was in his company or present for this meeting either.

She nodded a greeting since there was no need to curtsy.

De La Beche strode to the bell pull, his heels rapping on the flooring.

"Refreshments?" he asked, cocking one imperious brow.

Bryston glanced at Branwen, but she shook her head.

"No' for me, thank ye," she said, finding her way to a comfortable looking, velvet-covered sofa before the roaring fire in the hearth. She sank onto the cushion and primly folded her hands in her lap, welcoming the heat.

She'd grown chilled on the journey here.

Both in body and in spirit.

How would Bryston proceed?

He hadn't discussed his intentions with her.

"Please, Captain." De La Beche swept his hand outward, indicating Bryston should also sit.

Once they'd all claimed a seat, De La Beche placed one palm on a knee while gripping his cane with the other. The sapphire twinkled almost merrily. He looked between Branwen and Bryston. "Well, what's this all about then?"

In short order, Bryston explained about Le Sauvage's obsession with the treasure Anne Foissey had claimed existed. He also informed the reformed swashbuckler that he'd fathered Delphine and that Le Sauvage had visciously murdered her.

That news elicited a strong reaction.

Blanching, the Frenchman sank against the plush upholstery of his chair and shook his head. "*Zut*, Anne never breathed a word to me, I swear."

She probably hadn't known she carried his child until he'd sailed from Tortuga.

Mouth turned down, he fingered the cane's handle. "And this poor murdered mademoiselle was your wife, Captain, *oui*? And my daughter?"

He shook his head with what appeared to be genuine consternation before, again, sliding an assessing sideways glance to Branwen.

Was he trying to determine precisely what her relationship to Bryston was?

Branwen merely returned his frank regard. She owed him no explanation.

"Aye," Bryston replied, the familiar flintiness edging into his voice that always appeared when he spoke of Delphine.

"My sincere condolences," De La Beche murmured.

"Le Sauvage is off his head," Bryston said. "I thought him dead these past five years until he turned up in Leith a fortnight ago. He believes the treasure is still out there to be claimed."

A derisive chuckle filled the room as De La Beche shook his head and scraped a hand over his neatly trimmed beard. He brought his gaze up to encompass the room. "This house belongs to my wife's family. She's a Dassault, one of the oldest and wealthiest families in France. You may find it difficult to believe, but ours was a love-match."

That raised him greatly in Branwen's estimation.

"I'd amassed a small fortune, 'tis true. But I wisely invested it many years ago. My wife is a woman of, shall we say, *high* expectations, and I refused to be completely reliant upon the

Dassaults' generosity." His attention veered to his family's portrait, and a hint of the calloused pirate he once was shadowed his face.

He turned that flinty gaze to Bryston. "You spoke of danger, Captain McPherson?"

Bryston nodded. "Le Sauvage is in Rouen. He's crazed enough that he may come here."

De La Beche slowly nodded. "I will alert my men to be extra diligent, but what purpose would that serve? Even if he'd intended to steal my plunder, it has long since been converted into more acceptable and respectable endeavors."

Bryston tapped his fingers upon his thigh before rolling a broad shoulder.

Must he do that?

How was a woman supposed to remain impervious to such overt masculinity?

"I dinna ken, in all honesty," Bryston admitted. "But as I've said, we arena dealin' with a rational man."

A movement caught the corner of her eye, and Branwen cast a disinterested glance to the terrace. Her blood ran cold with fear, and her heart palpitated in dread.

Nae. Nae.

Gasping, she clasped one hand to her throat just as Le Sauvage kicked a French window open.

Wearing that same ridiculous hat, the feathers waving an impertinent greeting, he strode inside, acting as if he were simply calling as an invited guest and hadn't just broken a door. For the first time, she noticed his flaming red boots.

The man had a penchant for red, it would seem.

Blackened teeth bared, a pair of filthy henchmen flanked him on each side. All wielded ugly swords. Their fetid body odor carried to her, several feet away, and she swallowed a gag.

Swiftly examining their weapons, relief washed over Branwen.

Praise the saints. Nae blood.

Hopefully, that meant they hadn't killed anyone. How had they sneaked past Bryston's men?

Bryston leaped to his feet, his boots thudding hard against the floor. At once, he seized his dirk and sword. In one fluid motion, he withdrew both, his stance defensive as he moved to guard Branwen.

De La Beche vaulted from his seat as well and slid a thin sword from his cane.

Och, verra clever.

The sensible former pirate hadn't met with Bryston unarmed after all.

She pulled her small dagger from the folds of her skirt, her attention fixed on the intruders.

The odds weren't with them: five to three. And with her small blade, she hardly counted.

Could she really use the dagger on a man?

Kill him, even?

She eyed the murderous pirates.

Aye, she believed she could.

"Now, De La Beche, *s'il vous plaît* tell me where you have hidden the treasure I have sought these many years, *oui*?" Le Sauvage purred, a sinister sneer twisting his features. He smoothed his hand over his beard.

De La Beche's only reaction was to elevate a sardonic eyebrow.

"The desire to claim it for myself is what kept me alive the four torturous years my men and I were pressed into service aboard the *Hell's Siren*," Le Sauvage continued conversationally. "We were little more than slaves after they plucked us from the Atlantic."

So that was where he'd been all this time.

She cast Bryston a sideways glance.

Jaw flexing, his fingers reflexively clenching and unclenching the handles of his weapons, pure hatred spewed from the murderous glare he directed at Le Sauvage. "And I presume ye talked the crew into mutinyin'?"

"*Oui*." Le Sauvage gave an indifferent shrug as he took in the room's lavishness. "When the captain was killed durin' a skirmish, 'twas only natural I should assume command of the ship, *non*?"

An evil grin contorted the pockmarked face of one of his men. "Aye, and Captain Le Sauvage might've hurried the bastard along to rot at the bottom o' the sea."

His comrades chuckled diabolically.

"What a surprise," drawled De La Beche drolly. Lifting his sword, he made a casual circle in the air. "Monsieur, I fear you are misinformed. *This* is my treasure. My home. My family." He thinned his mouth into a rueful line. "There truly is naught else."

He shook his head in false regret, an ominous threat of retribution glinting in his eyes.

"*Non*. I do not believe you." Hefting an exaggerated sigh, Le Sauvage swaggered forward a couple of steps, his men mirroring his movements.

Where in God's precious name where Bayu? Scags? Jabir?

"That *putain*, Anne Foissey, bragged about yer treasure. In her dyin' breath, her daughter mentioned it as well," Le Sauvage said.

"Like hell she did," Bryston roared, raising his weapons.

Le Sauvage pointed his sword at Bryston, and Branwen felt perspiration dampen her underarms. "*Tut, tut,* McPherson. The last time you lost your temper with me, I gave you that scar."

A feral growl echoed low in Bryston's throat, very much reminding Branwen of a wild creature cornered and prepared to fight to the death.

In truth, that analogy mightn't be so very far-fetched.

Le Sauvage's oily gaze gravitated to Branwen and lingered on her bosom. "I must admit, your taste in women is superb."

His lewd appraisal made Branwen's skin shrink, and she instinctively edged nearer to Bryston.

"Alas, Annie Foissey was a woman given to too much drink and an even greater imagination, *non*?" De La Beche murmured. "Any treasure spoken of during our acquaintance was of a...carnal nature." He veered Branwen a repentant glance. "My apologies for my indelicacy, Miss Glanville."

De La Beche had been a young pirate, sowing his proverbial wild oats. Likely, he'd never thought of Annie Foissey again once he'd sailed from Tortuga.

Le Sauvage languidly returned his focus to Bryston while tapping the tip of his sword on the floor, making a portentous *clink, clink, clink* sound.

"Ah, but the *belle* Delphine spoke of the treasure with her last breaths." He drew his eyebrows into an accusatory line. "She specifically said your name, McPherson, and uttered the word 'treasure.'"

"Ye goddamned bastard," Bryston thundered. "I called her *my* treasure. She wasn't speakin' of baubles and jewels and coins and other bloody meanin'less rot. She meant love and adoration, somethin' ye obviously ken nothin' of."

Branwen's heart broke for him as he faced his wife's murderer. The poor woman's last words had been of her love for Bryston. Stinging tears pricked behind her eyelids.

It shattered Branwen as she fully understood the depths of his love for Delphine and hers for him.

Och, to be loved so wholly and devotedly by a man such as he.

Le Sauvage's confidence faltered, and a flicker of uncertainty danced across his sun-bronzed features. He narrowed his snake-like eyes, his attention traveling from De La Beche to Bryston and back to De La Beche.

A wholly humorless grin edged Bryston's mouth upward. "That's why ye had a spy infiltrate Trentwick Castle, isna it? Because ye think I kent where the treasure was?"

Branwen shot him an astonished glance.

Spy? At Trentwick?

"Christ, ye're as stupid as a neep," Bryston said.

His upper lip curled in anger at the insult, another gleam of uncertainty flashed in Le Sauvage's eyes.

That mocking grin still in place, Bryston canted his head and gave a derisive snort. "Yer spy is as much an idiot as ye. He told ye there is somethin' between this lass and I too, didna he?"

He inclined his head toward her, his flaxen hair swinging with the movement.

Something unhinged in Branwen's heart at the cold, dismissive way he uttered those indifferent words, but she refused to let her devastation show on her face. Instead, she straightened her spine and arranged her features into controlled disdain.

She swung her blade side to side.

"Well, now that is a colossal mistake. A most embarrassin' and incompetent one. Mr. McPherson has been assigned to be my bodyguard at the behest of my guardian. I've known him since I was a young lass. There is absolutely *nothin'* between us. Nor will there ever be."

THIRTEEN

Bryston kept his warrior-honed attention focused on the blackguard only a few feet away from Branwen, but her adamant declaration shredded his heart.

And he'd stupidly believed he'd grown numb to pain.

Now, however, wasn't the time to ruminate upon her statement, because if he didn't miss his mark, Bayu and the others would appear at any moment, and hell was about to break loose.

"Branwen," he warned to alert her just as a shadow slanted across the terrace.

A heartbeat later, his men exploded inside. In the ensuing chaos, shouts, curses, screams of pain, and the violent striking of blade upon blade, he had but one thought.

Protect Branwen.

He *must,* at all costs, protect Branwen.

God's bones, he couldn't see another woman he loved die.

Love?

Aye, by damn. Love.

He loved the silver-eyed beauty.

So caught up with the epiphany, he forgot to defend

himself for a heartbeat. Le Sauvage's triumphant snarl hurtled Bryston back to the present. He swung his sword, barely deflecting a punishing blow by one of the assling's beefy crewmen.

Shite.

Pay attention!

Of all the inopportune times to realize and admit he did love Branwen, it had to be when her life was in danger yet again? Except, this time, Le Sauvage would not take the woman Bryston loved from him.

As Bryston anticipated he would, Le Sauvage went straight for Branwen. The bastard enjoyed killing women and children. Far easier prey then fighting men.

Rather than cower or shriek in terror, she adjusted her grip on the dagger. Eyes narrowed to slits and her lips a thin ribbon of concentration, with a practiced twist of her wrist, she sent the blade sailing through the air to impale his shoulder.

I'll be damned.

Bryston couldn't check his grin of astonished approval.

It seemed Keane had trained his wards to protect themselves, and he'd been worried Branwen wouldn't know how to use the blade.

Stupefied, the pirate gazed down at the silver handle protruding from him, then raised his murderous gaze to her. "*Merde.* You'll pay for that, mademoiselle. *Oui*, you will. When I'm done carving your pretty face, no one will recognize you."

Clutching the grip, he yanked the knife from his flesh and tossed it onto the floor where it landed with a hollow clank and skidded a couple of feet.

At once, Branwen whirled away, searching for another weapon to defend herself.

That was all the time Bryston needed to put himself between Branwen and Le Sauvage.

Blood oozing from the gash in his chest, the madman didn't appear to feel any pain. He screamed, the sound piercing and deranged, as he lunged for Bryston.

With every arc and swing of his blades, Bryston cursed the man to hell a thousand times over. Wrought the devil's vengeance for Delphine with every lancing blow he dealt the pirate. And most of all, battled unrelentingly to defend the magnificent woman whose soul was the other half of his.

Branwen scurried out of the way of the fighting men and stood hovering beside the fireplace, a poker gripped in her hands in much the same way one would wield a sword.

By damn, did she know how to do that as well?

Finally, with a rotation and a thrust, while simultaneously clobbering Le Sauvage upon the side of the head with his fist, Bryston wrested the man's weapon from his grip. The last of his men to be disarmed, Le Sauvage's weapon dropped with a loud, reverberating, and wholly fulfilling *thunk* upon the wood floor.

Chest heaving and his breathing labored, Bryston swiftly assessed the others.

His men hadn't come through the scuffle untainted.

Three suffered multiple gashes but remained on their feet, crimson oozing between the fingers clasping their wounds. Scags lay insensate, a small pool of congealing blood spreading out from beneath the side of his head.

However, two of Le Sauvage's men stared sightlessly at the ceiling, another writhed upon the floor moaning and clutching hands to his bloodied abdomen, and the fourth poltroon had fled.

His hat long since trampled underfoot, whistling gasps expanding his chest, and perspiration streaming down his reddened face, Le Sauvage staggered, the tips of Bryston's, De La Beche's, and Jabir's swords at his convulsing throat.

Though his sword lay upon the ground, in his outstretched left hand, he clenched a dagger reflexively.

"On yer knees," Bryston gritted out, prodding the cur with his weapon and drawing a thin line of scarlet across Le Sauvage's throat.

With a half-groan, half-oath, the pirate fell heavily onto his knees, insanity and hatred glowing in his eyes.

"You think you've won, *non*?" he spat.

"Aye, ye bloody bastard, I have," Bryston allowed with no small amount of satisfaction.

Wordlessly, the pirate glared at him, then turned his loathing toward Branwen. His lip curled as he cursed. "If it weren't for the bitch, the outcome would've been much different, McPherson, *non*?"

Perhaps. Perhaps not.

After returning the poker to its place, Branwen skirted them, her gaze leery and alert. She kneeled beside Scags and examined him, making a soft sound of empathy in her throat. She withdrew a frilly handkerchief from her pocket and pressed it to the side of his head.

Scags would not be pleased to learn that feminine bit of cloth staunched his wound. He'd consider it unmanly. Better to bleed to death than be coddled.

He groaned, and his eyelids fluttered open.

"Am I in heaven?" he croaked weakly, using the opportunity to look his fill at the mounds of Branwen's full breasts only a few inches away.

"*Scags...*" Bryston warned silkily, jealousy turning his voice gravelly.

Branwen seemed oblivious to his possessiveness as she tutted and fretted over the Scot.

Jabir released a full-bodied chuckle, and Bayu said, "'Tis doubtful that is where you will find yourself when you pass from this world, my friend."

Scags glowered and raised a fist in feigned anger.

"Hold still, Mr. Scags," Branwen told him as she accepted the cloth Jabir had removed from around his neck and folded into a square. She applied it to the wound as well. "Ye've a nasty cut on yer scalp. I canna be certain, but I think ye'll need stitches."

Assured Branwen was safe, and Scags would survive, Bryston returned his regard to Le Sauvage. Casting De La Beche a sideways glance, his hand yet gripping his sword, he said, "Send someone for the authorities."

By God, how he longed to take Le Sauvage's life himself. Torture the cowardly dog as he'd tortured Delphine. But he grudgingly acknowledged that would make him no better than the piece of excrement kneeling before him.

A fortnight ago, he would've done so without a qualm, damning the consequences to ten times Sunday. But Branwen... *Aye, Branwen.* She'd made him see the goodness in the world again. He wanted to be worthy of her. Of her love.

With a sharp nod, De La Beche turned to the doorway where three terrified servants huddled. The butler brandished a candelabra, one footman held a bed warmer, and the other footman clutched what appeared to be a mop.

Bryston almost rolled his eyes at the ludicrousness but didn't want to humiliate the cowering trio.

"Tasse?" De La Beche addressed the waxen-faced major-domo. "Picard and Vettel are to go for the magistrate and a physician at once, *non*? Did you send for the men to come up from the village, as I asked you to if there was any trouble?"

"Indeed, sir. I am surprised they haven't arrived as yet." At once, the butler turned to the footmen and rapidly issued orders in French. Relief washing over their ashen faces at not being required to defend their master with household items, they promptly trotted away to do his bidding.

Tasse turned his soulful-eyed, offended scrutiny to the broken furniture, blood-smeared flooring, shattered vases and whatnots, and lashed curtains. He swayed noticeably on his feet. "*Mon Dieu*. Madame will be most distressed."

Aye, but she'd be grateful her husband was alive.

"Is there someplace this bastard can be held until the magistrate arrives?" Bryston asked, plucking the dagger from Le Sauvage's fingers.

Bayu lowered his weapon, but Jabir kept his sword tip nestled against the pirate's jugular.

"*Oui*." Nodding, De La Beche said, "There is a window-less servant's accommodation with a stout door below." Once more, he turned to his fussing butler in the process of gingerly stepping over scarlet droplets.

Appearing about to weep upon spying a broken clock, he touched a knuckle to the corner of one eye. "It was a *Religieuse*," he bemoaned beneath his breath.

"Tasse, please show the captain's men where they can secure Le Sauvage," directed De La Beche, sympathy softening his timbre.

Shaking his head ruefully, Tasse exhaled an exaggerated sigh. "This way, please."

After tying Le Sauvage's hands behind his back with De Le Beche's swiftly proffered neckcloth, Jabir and Bayu towed the struggling, foully swearing Le Sauvage from the room.

"He will hang, of course," De La Beche stated dispassionately, toeing aside a blue and white ceramic shard. "I will see to it as retribution for my daughter's murder."

Delphine would've liked her father had she ever met him.

Bryston held his gaze for an extended moment before dipping his chin in acquiescence.

"I should hope so," Branwen said vehemently as she helped Scags into an upright position. "He's too vile to live."

Two bright spots of color tinted her cheeks.

Bryston noticed she studiously avoided meeting his gaze, and he burned to tell her what she'd longed to hear. What he'd only just discovered himself when it was almost too late. To whisper the words into her delicate ear and watch the joy transform her features.

Nae yet.

Nae in a room full of dead and wounded men.

De La Beche wiped her dagger blade clean, then extended it to her. An approving smile tipped his mustached mouth upward.

"I am most impressed at your skill, mademoiselle. *Mon Dieu*, never have I seen a woman throw a blade with such accuracy." He winked, and jealousy winged through Bryston's middle again. "My wife would've fainted when the pirates burst in. Ever so gracefully, of course."

"I dinna faint." Flicking a glance at the shattered French window, Branwen chuckled. "My guardian believes it is important for women to be able to defend themselves."

Her expression sobered, and she eyed the weapon with distaste before sighing, grudgingly accepting it, and returning it to the sheath hidden in the folds of her skirts.

"I must concur. Perhaps I can persuade my wife to permit our Solène to learn the art." De La Beche narrowed his eyes thoughtfully. He turned to Bryston. "You must stay here tonight, *mon ami*. It will be hours before the magistrate arrives, and our captive is dealt with appropriately."

"Nae." Bryston declined with a slight shake of his head. "Have the magistrate call at the *Hôtel De La Rouen* on the morrow to take our statements. However, I would appreciate ye seein' to my wounded men and their transport back to Rouen. I'd like to weigh anchor as soon as possible. Miss Glanville's guardian is most anxious for her return."

Something akin to pain flashed across Branwen's features before she schooled her features and shifted her focus from him. Damn, she probably thought he was eager to see her home after their quarrel in the carriage.

Impatience chafed him. He couldn't explain anything with extra people about listening in. When he revealed his feelings, it wouldn't be surrounded by death and gore. She should be courted and wooed. Made to feel cherished and adored.

"Is that safe, McPherson?" De La Beche queried, bending to pick up a white Madonna marble sculpture that had, incredibly, survived the destruction.

"Jabir and Bayu will return with us. I doubt the rest of Le Sauvage's crew is as loyal as these curs." He dropped his gaze to the dead and wounded pirates. "The scunner who fled will tell them of their captain's capture and imminent execution, and I'd wager they commandeer the *Hell's Siren* for themselves," he told De La Beche.

"Hmm, you have a valid point," De La Beche acknowledged.

"Do ye have capable men who can guard Le Sauvage?" Bryston asked.

De La Beche swung his gaze to look out the broken door. "I do. I've already sent for them. As Tasse mentioned, they should've arrived by now."

Then why hadn't they been in place beforehand?

Perhaps De La Beche hadn't thought there was a need. It might've saved a degree of bloodshed.

As if reading Bryston's mind, he said, "Madame De La Beche would prefer no reminders of my former life, or else I'd have a half-dozen guards ensconced in the house and stables. I considered sending for my men this morning but rightly assumed you'd bring your own." He lifted his shoulder as he ran his gaze over the demolished room. "I didn't think a man who would warn me I was in danger would then cause me harm."

De La Beche had become too trusting in his retirement from piracy, but Bryston refrained from saying so.

Just then, a quartet of very capable, burly men plowed into the room. De La Beche crossed to them and spoke in soft tones. After casting inquisitive glances at Bryston and Branwen, they departed, led by their employer.

Bryston took Branwen's elbow, and she didn't flinch away from him, but she did give him a doubtful look.

"Come, let's return to Rouen. We've much to discuss," he said quietly.

Angling her head, she searched his face while disengaging her arm from his hand.

"Nae, Bryston. We've had our discussion already. There's naught else left to say."

Without a backward glance, she sailed from the room.

FOURTEEN

Five hours later
Hôtel De La Rouen

Weary to her core, Branwen ran the brush Bryston had purchased for her through her hair. Closing her eyes, she pondered the past few hours. The return journey to Rouen had been much the same as that to *Châteaux de Beaumont.*

With the exception of one predominate thing—one undeniably painful thing.

She'd been a starry-eyed lass with hopes of love on the way there.

That was no longer the case, and she couldn't summon an ounce of anger or censure.

How could she possibly begrudge Bryston his love for Delphine?

She refused to permit jealousy or envy a foothold. Such were direct paths to bitterness, acrimony, and discontent. Nae, Branwen sincerely respected his loyalty and commitment, even this many years after his wife's death.

Today, not only had Branwen realized she and Bryston

could never be, but she'd also stabbed a man and witnessed the deaths of others.

True, Le Sauvage was as rotten and misbegotten a scunner—a devil's spawn, if there ever was one—as they came. In all of the times she'd trained with Keane, she'd never expected to actually have to use a blade against another person.

Had her actions truly made a difference?

Aye, she believed they had, and she couldn't deny the self-confidence and pride that knowledge aroused in her. Though it hadn't even been a fortnight ago, she'd changed since fleeing Leith.

Having lived in her older sister's shadow and with an exceedingly protective guardian since she was a wee lass, she'd discovered she was much stronger and more independent than she'd previously believed. And, by heaven, she liked that about herself. It gave her the confidence to forge her own future.

Aye, she might be returning to Trentwick Castle, but she'd do her utmost to persuade Keane and Marjorie to permit her to travel. She wasn't certain how that might be accomplished since neither enjoyed traveling themselves, but perhaps a companion could be hired. A distant relative imposed upon. She would find a means.

And she'd take up a cause or hobby too, though, in truth, she wasn't quite certain what that would be.

Branwen only had one life to live, and she wouldn't spend it pining for a wonderful man. Oh, her heart and soul would always belong to Bryston, but that didn't mean she couldn't pull up her stockings and get on with it.

Unrequited love was tragic but not the end of the world. Far more heart-rending to her way of thinking would be to waste the life the Lord had given her. To not seize every opportunity and experience she was able to.

With a firm nod, not quite having convinced herself,

Branwen puffed out a sigh. She set the brush beside the hair-pins and the letter to post to Marjorie and Keane tomorrow that rested on the dressing table. Slowly, reluctantly, she brought her gaze to meet her reflection in the looking glass.

She gave a sharp little shake of her head and pursed her lips at what she saw there.

Sorrow. Resignation. Discouragement.

Those were what shadowed the eyes, the color of the North Sea in January, mirrored back at her.

Well, little steps, she assured herself.

She couldn't very well expect a pulverized heart to heal in mere hours, could she?

Bryston had respected her muffled request not to converse on the way back to Rouen, and she'd dozed off only to awaken as the carriage lurched to a halt in the hotel's courtyard. Unable to bear her own doleful expression and more drained emotionally and physically than at any other time she could recall, she stood and wandered to the window.

Freshly bathed and her hair washed, she'd barely touched her dinner. Now, though it was not even seven of the clock, she considered crawling into bed and pulling the bedding over her head. If only it were that simple to snuff her tumultuous thoughts.

Slumber, at least, would obliterate her heartache for a brief while.

The magistrate had sent word he'd meet with her and Bryston in the morning, and she'd overheard him telling Bayu to ready *The Dolphin* to set sail tomorrow evening.

Good.

She was homesick.

Heartsick too.

Knock. Knock. Knock.

Scrunching her brow, she checked the tie of her robe before calling, "Who is it?"

"Nanette, Miss Glanville," burbled the cheery maid in her heavy accent through the door. "You have a delivery."

A delivery?

What in the world?

Branwen opened the door a crack, well aware of the impropriety of doing so wearing her nightclothes.

A delighted grin dominated the lower half of the plump girl's face. Holding a vase containing a huge bouquet of flowers, she bobbed her head at six other maids behind her.

Each held a box wrapped in pretty fabric and festooned with a large ribbon. Except for the last, who cooed and patted an acorn-brown, curly-coated puppy.

Puzzling her brow, completely baffled, Branwen gazed helplessly at the array before her. "Are ye certain ye havena made a mistake?" Her attention gravitated to the beaming maids. "This is all meant for me?"

Giving an exuberant nod, Nanette giggled as she and her cohorts exchanged knowing glances. "'Tis wondrous, *non?*"

"Aye," Branwen agreed.

Perhaps it was De La Beche's way of saying thank you? Or his wife's?

Overwhelmed, Branwen stepped aside and permitted the servants to parade into the chamber proudly bearing the gifts.

Nanette placed the bouquet on the table beside Branwen's nearly full dinner tray. She tsked upon spying the uneaten food. "You did not like the meal, mademoiselle? Shall I bring you something else? *Oui?*" she asked, so eager to please.

"I didn't have much of an appetite after the events of the day," Branwen consoled, not wanting to hurt the servant's feelings. Witnessing men die, impaling one herself, and relinquishing any hope of a future with Bryston had rather put her off her food. "Please dinna take offense. I'm sure on the morrow I'll be famished."

"*Oui*, fresh croissants." Nanette put her fingertips to her mouth and made a kissing noise.

The other excited maids placed their boxes on the bed.

"The puppy is a female. If she needs to go outside, just ring, and someone will come up to take her out," Nanette offered with a little, shallow curtsy.

"Arena you adorable?" Branwen said, accepting the wriggling puppy from a maid whose name she did not know. It promptly began licking her face enthusiastically. Despite her earlier melancholy, she laughed and buried her nose in the dog's soft neck.

Holding the chubby, wriggling pup close, she took in the packages. "Do ye ken who they are from?"

"From me, lass."

She whirled to face Bryston, and her heart did that weird skittering, wobbly thing it always did when she looked upon him. Unabashedly, she permitted her gaze to feast upon his masculine magnificence.

Hair damp and hanging around his shoulders rather than tied back at the sides as was his wont and wearing only a linen shirt, leather breeches, and boots, his large frame dominated the doorframe. Arms folded, he rested one ridiculously broad shoulder against the wood.

He winked at the maids who erupted into giggles once more.

"Mademoiselles." He stepped aside, then bowed as he swept his arm out to indicate they should leave.

Falling over themselves while tittering and speaking in French—a couple of the bolder lasses giving Bryston seductive, inviting looks—they filed from the chamber.

Branwen waited until the last one's footsteps receded before speaking.

"Why? I havena need of anythin'. Ye've already purchased much for me that stretches the bounds of propriety." Branwen shook her head while trying to control the exuberant puppy. She was also aware the servants could still hear their conversation.

Clasping the back of his neck, he peered at her almost sheepishly and slanted his molded mouth into a disarming smile.

"I'm wooein' ye, Branwen. But because we're short on time, I'm acceleratin' the process. I figure a gift a week added to the near fortnight since we left Leith, that's almost two full moons of courtship."

She honed in on two words. Two glorious, terrifying, hope-stirring words.

Dinna become too excited.

Wooin' and lovin' are nae the same thing.

"Wooing me?" Eyes narrowed dubiously, she sniffed the air for the odor of spirits. "Are ye drunk?" she asked warily.

Was that what he'd been doing these past several hours? He didn't seem pished, but what other reason could there be for his impulsiveness?

His mouth bent into that sensual smile, and he closed the door. As always, his presence seemed to shrink the room.

Branwen resisted the urge to retreat a step for every one he advanced toward her. Instead, she planted her feet and angled her chin upward. The Branwen of old would've backed away, but the new Branwen faced things head-on.

"Aye." He took the puppy from her and ruffled its neck before placing it on the floor.

The roly-poly imp promptly pounced upon the carpet laid

before the hearth. It seized the edge in its little jaws, growling and shaking the undeserving carpet as if it were a rat.

A smile twitching her mouth at the puppy's antics, she placed her hands on her hips and scrutinized Bryston.

A devilish gleam glinted in his eyes as if he were privy to a secret.

"Bryston McPherson, what are ye about?"

He slashed her a roguish grin while wrapping those strapping arms around her waist and drawing her near. She should resist, but how could she, when with every breath, every beat of her heart, her every pore cried out for him?

"I brought ye sweetmeats, jewels, books, a small saber, a compass, and a mariner's astrolabe." He nuzzled her hair while flattening his palms against her upper and lower spine, pressing her flush against him.

God, he smelled heavenly, and she bit her lip to keep from nuzzling her nose into the open vee of his shirt. Whatever soap he'd used for bathing had left a spicy, woodsy essence on his sun-kissed skin.

Every rigid contour of his body—the sinewy thighs, the corded steps of his stomach, and the rock-solid bulges of his chest—reminded her how very different their bodies were. His hard, sculpted, and powerful. Hers, softer and rounder, and inviting.

"Bryston...?"

She battled to form his name, to draw enough oxygen into her lungs.

The physical effect he had on her was heady, a dizzying cacophony of sensation.

"Whatever would I do with a compass or a mariner's astrolabe?" she finally managed, her voice throaty with desire.

Whatever the latter was.

Branwen supposed it must be a nautical device of some sort.

"Sail around the world with me, Branwen." A husky timbre entered his voice as he stared into her eyes.

Why, there are gold flecks in his eyes.

How had she never noticed that before?

"Or explore the Himalayas," he continued, each word a throaty rumbling invitation. "Or teach our children the constellations."

Her breath hitched, suspended for a long, long sliver of a moment.

Is he sayin'?

She blinked back the sudden surge of tears—afraid to hope. To believe.

Tilting her head, she met his smoldering gaze.

"I love ye, Branwen." He brushed a calloused thumb across her cheek.

Her mouth parted in astonishment.

He pressed a hard kiss to the knuckles of one hand, then groaned and encompassed her in a powerful hug, wrapping those iron-like arms around her.

"I love ye. When I saw Le Sauvage turn to attack ye, I kent in that instant that I couldna envision the rest of my life without ye in it. Please, marry me."

"Och, Bryston, I love ye too." Branwen stood on her tiptoes and flung her arms around Bryston's neck, peppering his chin and jaw with kisses. "Aye, I'll wed ye."

He swooped her into his arms and, in three long strides, approached the bed.

She glanced over his shoulder. The puppy had given up attacking the rug and lay curled in a ball, sleeping soundly before the fire.

"Lass?" His voice and eyes held a question. "I will wait until we are wed if that is what ye wish."

Heat suffused her cheeks, but she shook her head. "Nae. We can marry tomorrow, but tonight I'd give myself to ye in the way a woman does a man. If ye promise me one thing, Bryston."

"Aye, anything lass." Such tenderness softened his eyes that tears sprang to hers.

"Ye will nae leave me behind. Where ye go, I go."

A smile teased his mouth before he swept it across hers. "Another bargain?"

"Aye." She grinned, tossing her hair over her shoulders. "I dinna intend to mind the hearth while ye roam the seas."

"It will be as ye wish, *leannán*. My heart beats with the fullness of ye, *mo chridhe*." *My heart.* "The blood running through my veins hums yer name."

If she hadn't already been in love with him, that vow would've catapulted her into falling in love all over again.

He gently deposited her on the bed, causing the packages to rustle and tumble. "Do ye want to open yer gifts first?"

She sliced the boxes a swift glance.

Nae, she didn't.

A wicked glint entered his eyes. "Before I open mine?"

"Nae, they can wait." She laughed and shook her head. "I canna."

While he moved the packages to the table with the bouquet, she removed her wrapper and lay it at the foot of the bed before turning the bedclothes down and climbing onto the bed. Biting her lip, she decided to leave her night rail on.

Branwen might be bolder than she was a few days ago, but maidenly modesty still prevailed.

She wanted this more than she'd ever wanted anything in her life. Wanted to become Bryston's woman. His wife.

Holding her gaze, a lazy smile arcing his mouth, he swiftly undressed.

Good Lord above.

She raked an appreciative gaze over him, admiring the delicious masculine architecture. All sinewy contours and rippling muscles. He was bloody magnificent, and his erect maleness, hard and proud, raised toward the rigid bands of his belly.

Swallowing, she brought her attention up to meet his eyes. Opening her arms, she invited him to her.

Then he was upon her, his length pressed against hers from toe to chest. Hunger swirled through her in heady waves. Bryston's hands and mouth were everywhere as he whispered words of love and desire.

She floated on a dizzying cloud of want and need and love.

When he entered her, so much joy sluiced through Branwen that tears leaked from the corners of her eyes.

"Branwen? Love?" Balanced on his elbows, he brushed her hair from her face. "We can stop if it pains ye too much."

"Nae. Nae. Dinna ever stop." She shook her head, clutching him to her breasts.

"Why are ye cryin'?" he asked, brushing his rough fingertips across her collarbone and causing little jolts of pleasure to spark outward.

"Because I'm so happy." She smiled into his eyes. "I'm so verra happy, Bryston."

His answering smile melted her heart, and she suspected she'd spend the rest of her life falling in love with him over and over and over.

He began to move then, slow, languid strokes, and with each surge, she rose higher and higher, her love carrying her to an ethereal place where only the two of them existed.

"I love ye," he moaned, his movements becoming stronger

and more insistent, driving the burning need inside her to new heights. "I love ye."

He raised her legs so that they encircled his waist, and a hissing gasp escaped between her parted lips.

"I love ye," she cried, as bliss shattered over her in undulating waves, so powerful that she felt faint. Before the last ripple ebbed, he stiffened and groaned, then pulled out to spurt his seed onto her belly.

"When we are married, I'll spill my seed in ye, but until then, I dinna want to chance to impregnate ye." He kissed her shoulder, then wiped her belly with the edge of the sheet before pulling her into his embrace.

Several minutes later, when reality settled upon Branwen once more, she sighed and snuggled closer to his side, draping a thigh across his hairy ones. "I think we'll have to wait to marry."

He cracked an eyelid open, his mouth turned down the merest bit. "Because?"

"Because I want my family present."

A blond eyebrow arched. "Aye, and we'll be at Trentwick within a fortnight."

Playing her fingers through the soft hair upon his chest, she shook her head. "Nae, I think I'd like to sail to the Caribbean first. I've heard it's verra warm and has beautiful beaches."

"Lass, Keane—"

She put two fingers to his lips and gave him what she hoped was a come-hither look. "Has nae way of kennin' how long it took us to rid ourselves of Le Sauvage."

Bryston grinned, a wicked bend of his mouth that had her imagining all sorts of naughty things he might do with those lips. Sweeping his hands down to cradle her hips, he murmured, "I'm sure we can reach an accord. I am, after all, quite adept at striking bargains."

Allowing him to pull her beneath him, she whispered, "I'm sure we can, my love. I'm thinking Portugal after the Caribbean..."

EPILOGUE

Early October 1728
Dunnancrief Manor
Scottish Highlands

High-pitched, quickly shushed giggles carried to Bryston as he strode into Dunnancrief Manor's entry. Ah, his bairns were playing their usual game when he arrived home after being away for a day or two.

Checking a grin, he covertly eyed the entrance.

Nae place for mischievous imps to hide here.

"Is my wife in the solar?" he asked Stoute, passing his cap and sword to the butler.

"Aye, sir."

Scarcely an inch over five feet tall, the majordomo nonetheless ran the household with military precision. Except for when it came to the trio of impish McPherson offspring. Those urchins he doted upon, and they could do no wrong in the crusty bachelor's eyes.

His gaze snapping with merriment, and eyebrows shied to his dusty red hairline, Stoute cleared his throat as he made an exaggerated visual search of the area. "Though I have *nae* idea where the bairns have disappeared to."

A happy yap, promptly followed by a loud "Shh," revealed that six-year-old Meddy and Alba, the mixed-breed mongrel Bryston had given Branwen over seven years ago, were nearby. Probably hiding behind the door to the dining room, given the slight creak of the walnut panel.

Better have that oiled, else a good hiding spot would be spoiled.

And since Meddy no doubt peeked at Bryston through the crack between the door and the doorframe, the smothered giggles came from Eliot and Errol.

Footsteps echoed on the floor a moment before Branwen appeared around the corner, her distended belly leading the way. A radiant smile bloomed across her face upon seeing him. "My love, ye *are* home. I thought I heard yer voice."

She came into his embrace as naturally and easily as a glove slid onto a hand or a foot into a shoe. They'd always fit together, and in the years since making her his wife, he'd come to know a love that surpassed that which he'd experienced with Delphine.

His first wife would always be a cherished memory, but Branwen had given him a reason for living again and fulfilled him in a way he'd not have believed possible.

The bairn in her belly chose that moment to kick, and she laughed.

"A feisty rascal, isna he?" Bryston chuckled as he placed his palm over her rounded stomach. "Ye are well, lass?"

Though he'd been away less than forty-eight hours, he'd missed her. Each day they grew closer, their very spirits fused, to the point she often finished his sentences and he knew her thoughts.

A small grimace pulled her pink mouth down and caused

two neat creases across her forehead. "I am, but I confess that though I have two months until the wee one arrives, I feel I could burst." She lifted quicksilver eyes to him, and he recognized a hint of apprehension swirling in their depths. "Ye dinna think 'tis twins again?"

What were the odds of that?

Unease lanced him, but he feigned nonchalance.

"What a gift that would be," Bryston soothed, his mind already scrambling to put a plan in place if that were the case again. During a breech birth, they'd almost lost Errol. As a result, the lad possessed a slight limp. "Dinna fash yerself, *jo*. We'll prepare for twins, just in case."

"Hmm." She made a noncommittal sound in her throat.

If he could take her place, he would spare her the suffering and angst.

Draping an arm around her shoulder, Bryston guided her toward her favorite place in the house—the solar. The many treasures they'd collected on their sojourns in the first year of marriage were proudly displayed there.

All the while, he watched for sneak attacks from his offspring.

Bryston had the addition built for Branwen when they'd returned to Scotland. They'd sailed the world after their wedding. However, once Branwen was increasing, she'd wanted to settle down and create a home for their bairn.

"What have ye done with my bairns?" Bryston casually asked.

"Why, I have nae idea where they are." Branwen made a pretense of looking flummoxed as she gazed around. "Surely, they must be nearby. They've been so verra eager to see their da."

Another stifled giggle floated from the alcove farther along the corridor, and the sea-foam green drapery fluttered the merest bit.

"Och, 'tis too bad Meddy, Eliot, and Errol arena here. I brought gifts home for them," Bryston said.

The three exploded from their hiding places, dashing straight toward their parents. Meddy had his hair but her mother's gray eyes. The boys had inherited Branwen's raven-black hair, but their eyes were a startling blue. Branwen said her father's eyes had been blue.

"Da, ye have a gift for us?" Meddy asked, her best friend panting at her side. The two had been inseparable since Alba first laid eyes on the lass.

"What is it, Da?" Errol asked, holding his brother's hand. "A sword?"

"A dagger? Dirk?" Grinning, Eliot swiped his hair off his forehead.

Someone had been filling his son's head with stories about pirates and buccaneers again.

Branwen gave him a contrite look and a half-shrug. "'Tis how I get them to fall asleep when ye are nae home. I tell them about yer adventures."

Bryston cleared his throat. "Ahem. Och, well."

He did not like the idea of his sons and daughter following in those footsteps.

Meddy laid a small hand on Branwen's belly and leaned in to speak to the infant. "Hello, wee bairn. Please be a lass." She cut her brothers, now pretending to sword fight, an impatient glance. "I'm already outnumbered."

Branwen took her hand. "Well, if we count Alba, there are three lasses and three laddies."

For a moment, Bryston thought their daughter might be mollified, but after a few seconds, she shook her head. "Nae, I love Alba, but she canna talk to me."

Collecting one of his son's hands in each of his, he canted his head toward the butler.

Stoute smiled fondly as he opened the door Bryston had passed through not more than five minutes ago.

"Close yer eyes," Bryston told his children.

Obediently, they shut their eyes as he and Branwen led them outside.

Alba barked excitedly, and the children's eyelids popped open.

Three sturdy Shetland ponies stood in a neat row, a groom holding each by a harness.

"Ponies!" The twins whooped in unison, jumping up and down.

"Da, we *each* get one?" Wide-eyed in wonderment, Meddy clapped her hands.

"Bryston, why dinna ye tell me?" Branwen gave him a reproachful look, her brilliant smile belying any true censure.

"The gray one is for Meddy, the black for Eliot, and the bay for Errol." He'd decided on the way home it was better to not let the children choose. Meddy's was slightly larger, and Errol's was the most docile.

" Can ye calmly approach them?" he asked, looking to his sons and then Meddy. "Ye dinna want to scare them."

"Aye, Da," they chorused.

Bryston released the boys' hands, and Branwen released Meddy's.

As their children greeted the ponies, he drew his wife to his side. "I have something for ye too."

She gazed at him with adoration, and his heart plopped at her feet.

"Ye ken I dinna need trinkets and baubles."

"This isna a trinket or a bauble."

He angled his head to the end of the drive.

She turned her attention in that direction and gasped, putting a hand to her throat and tears welled in her eyes. "Och, Bryston. She's lovely."

A stable hand brought a majestic white mare with a black mane and tail forward.

"The moment I saw her, I kent she was for you. Her name is Starlight, but ye canna ride until after the bairn is born." He drew her near, kissing her sweet mouth. "Happy birthday, love."

"But my birthday isna for a fortnight." Branwen started to move toward the mare, but he grasped her hand.

"I have another surprise for ye."

It had taken a good bit of corresponding and secretive arranging, but he'd managed to contrive to have her family present for her birthday too.

"Ye are too good to me," she said softly, love shining in her eyes.

"Branwen." Her sister emerged from behind a bush.

Tears trailed down Branwen's cheeks, and she wept openly as Bethea ran toward her, arms outstretched. Camden followed, carrying a toddler while a nurse urged two more sons after their father. Keane, Marjorie, her two daughters, and their other two children, all wearing grins, marched up the drive as well.

After exchanging hugs and kisses, the horseflesh secured in the stables, the children tucked into the nursery, and the adults shown to their rooms to freshen up before dinner, Bryston pulled Branwen into their bedchamber.

Eyes glowing, she raised on her toes and kissed him. "Ye've always been so thoughtful. I've missed my family so much."

"I ken ye have." He kissed her nose. "I might've invited a few more people to yer birthday celebration, lass."

She quirked a brow and leaned slightly away from him.

"How many precisely?"

He grinned and nuzzled her fragrant neck. "Graeme Kennedy and his family, the McGregors, Wallaces, Rutherfords, and the Catherwoods."

Her mouth slackened, and her eyes rounded. "Ye dinna."

"Aye, I did." He tilted her chin up, gazing deeply into her eyes. "We've all found true love, Branwen, and ye ken the heart of a Scot is nae easily given. I'd have our children and our friends' bairns see what love can accomplish. Who kens what the future of Scotland holds, but I ken that with ye, I can face anythin'?"

"And I with ye, husband."

If you'd like to leave a review, please scan the QR code.

Keep reading for a free preview of
A CHRISTMAS KISS FOR THE HIGHLANDER
Heart of a Scot Series, Book Nine

A CHRISTMAS KISS FOR THE HIGHLANDER

***Eytone Hall, Scottish Highlands
September 1720***

Cantering his horse up the well-maintained drive to Eytone Hall, Quinn felt the tension easing from his muscles. It had always been like this when he visited Liam MacKay, Baron Penderhaven, one of the few men he called a true friend. One of the very few people he trusted. The doors to Eytone Hall were open to him whenever he decided to drop in for an unannounced visit, and today would be no exception.

He called no place home, preferring the freedom to come and go at will. But if he had, Eytone Hall came the closest. In fact, Liam's mother, Lady Penderhaven, made certain his usual chamber was always prepared and his clothes hung inside the wardrobe—clean.

"Thank ye." Handing Benedict's reins off to the liveried footman who'd hurried from the grand mansion to attend the gelding, Quinn skewed his mouth into a grin. It truly was good to be here.

He untied his pack from the saddle while sending his gaze around the familiar courtyard and lands. Creamy, shorn sheep dotted one sloping hillside, and reddish-brown Highland cows milled about on another.

Even he could admit there was something enjoyable about the familiarity and comfort of returning to a place where he'd known a degree of contentment and peace. *Contentment? Peace?* That was a stretch, and neither were things he'd particularly coveted.

Until recently.

Nevertheless, if he didn't relish his freedom so much, he might envy Liam MacKay. Slinging his pack over one shoulder, he drew his mouth into a grim line. No, he didn't. Liam had been through bloody hell these past few years.

"Simmons." He nodded to the austere butler poised beside the mansion's double doors. "Ye're lookin' well."

Simmons angled his hoary head. "As are ye, Mr. Catherwood." He closed the doors, then reached for Quinn's satchel. "I'll have yer bag delivered to yer usual chamber."

"Thank ye. Is Liam at home?" More than once, Quinn had arrived to find Liam absent, not that he wasn't still made wholly welcome by Lady Penderhaven and her daughter, Kendra. He'd known that minx since she'd worn braids, and she was still inevitably embroiled in some sort of mischief or other.

"Nae, he isna, though he is expected back any day." He passed Quinn's pack to the footman before angling toward the corridor. "Will ye join her ladyship for tea at half past three?"

Quinn would rather lick the marble floor than perch on a settee and exchange trivial comments, but he summoned a droll smile, nevertheless. He was capable of acting the part of a gentleman. After all, he'd been raised as such, even if he'd chosen to leave that life behind a decade ago.

What time was it, anyway?

His pocket watch had been rather smashed on his last mission, and he hadn't replaced the timepiece yet. He didn't relish cooling his heels in the salon for an hour or two, waiting for the lady of the house's arrival when he could traipse about outside or enjoy a long relaxing soak in the tub while sipping a glass of Liam's superior cognac.

"Lead on, good fellow. I shall endeavor to appear civilized." He clasped a palm to his chest. "I promise no' to slurp my tea or chew with my mouth open."

He might talk with his mouth full though.

One of Simmons' wiry eyebrows shied upward the merest bit. *Ah, that's right.* The butler didn't possess a sense of humor.

No one in Baron Penderhaven's household had ever accused Quinn of being ungentlemanly or, for that matter, of being a gentleman. He skirted the bounds of propriety, not quite drifting so far astray as to be ostracized but never teetering over the edge into complete respectability either.

"Might I suggest ye freshen up first?" Nothing subtle about that or the butler's slightly flared nostrils.

Quinn was quite covered in dust, and he stank of sweat and horse.

"Indeed. An excellent notion." He swiveled toward the impressive staircase instead.

Twenty minutes later, he tripped back down the risers, having made do with the washstand water after examining the night table clock and finding it three-quarters past two. Just his blasted luck, he'd also nicked himself shaving in his haste. Putting a fingertip to the still-stinging cut, he checked for fresh blood.

Wouldn't do to bleed all over his starched neckcloth. He only had three here.

He passed the impressive library and had nearly gone beyond the drawing room when movement inside the open doorway caught his attention. Scrunching his brows together into a puzzled frown, he halted.

Hadn't Simmons said tea was to be served in the rose salon?

No, although that was where her ladyship generally preferred to take her tea, the butler hadn't specified where earlier. Mayhap things had changed since Quinn last visited. After all, it had been over six months. He pivoted and, touching his cut again, strode into the room.

A startlingly exquisite woman with glorious, pale honey-colored hair piled atop her head and attired in a white and robin's egg blue gown whirled away from the window. Her incredibly blue eyes widened, and she put a delicate hand to her throat where a single row of creamy pearls rested.

A long, intense minute stretched out, lengthening into something extraordinary and potent as they stared at each other, neither seeming able to break the inexplicable and imme-diate powerful connection which thrummed between them.

Good God. He almost expected choruses of *Hallelujah* and the harmony of violin strings to fill the sweetly tense atmosphere.

Finally, somehow marshaling his composure, he swept into a gallant's bow. Not usually at a loss for words or one to falter when faced with something unexpected—after all, his line of work tossed him in the middle of the perilous and unforeseen on a daily basis—he commanded his galloping pulse to return to its normal pace.

Opening his mouth, he found every drop of moisture had vanished. He cleared his throat, then swallowed. Blast, he was behaving more ineptly than a wet-behind-the-ears pup.

She remained statue-still, much like a wary doe prepared to flee if he moved suddenly.

"Please permit me to introduce myself. Quinn Catherwood, yer most humble servant, my lady." He found himself standing over her, not consciously recalling having moved across the carpet. The top of her shiny head reached his shoulder.

He envisioned leading her in a dance, or wrapping his arms about her delicate shoulders, or resting his cheek on the crown of her head. Yes, to all of that and more.

The girl was impossibly more perfect up close, her skin milky and smooth as silk. Navy-blue ringed her light azure irises framed by golden, winged brows. A delicate floral and citrus scent wafted upward from her sleek hair, and he inhaled her heady fragrance.

She was... *Odin's teeth.* She was—God help him—an answer to a prayer he hadn't even known he'd desired. And she must be his. *His.*

Gazing up at him, her peach-tinted lips slightly parted, she seemed as transfixed as he. As if coming to her senses, she blinked and lowered her hand to her waist.

"I'm Skye Hendron, Baron Penderhaven's cousin, visiting from England," she said in a melodious, cultured tone. "I'm simply a miss, not a lady."

Very proper and English, but not the least stuffy or superior. Her voice held an unexpected husky quality that immediately sent his senses into a spin once more.

"I'm most pleased I decided to pay my auld friend a visit." Quinn couldn't drag his focus from her exquisite features or the lively intelligence dancing in her amused gaze.

God's teeth.

His pulse leaped again. An extended stay might be in

order. No, most definitely was in order. "Will ye be here long?"

God and all the saints, please say aye.

A slight shadow passed over her features, tipping her lovely mouth downward as she directed her focus to the window behind him. "Truthfully, I'm not sure. My father has fallen ill, and my mother sent me to Eytone Hall while she tends him. I pray 'tis nothing serious." As if as an afterthought, she waved her hand gracefully. "Aunt Louisa is my mother's sister."

At her obvious distress, a strange coiling began in Quinn's middle, spreading outward until it tangled around his heart. How could he want to gather this woman in his arms and promise her she could rely upon him for...*what?*

Comfort? Protection? Security?

Aye. Aye, and much more.

Something he'd never considered until this very instant, but so wondrous that he'd be an absolute idiot not to pursue whatever *this* was.

"I'm sorry, lass. I'm sure ye'd rather be with them than here no' kennin' what is happenin'." He tipped his mouth into a compassionate arc. "It must weigh heavily on ye. Have ye any brothers or sisters?"

She pulled her vibrant gaze back, surprise and appreciation for his understanding shining in her eyes. "It does, and no. I am an only child."

So was he.

"Mr. Catherwood—"

"Quinn. Ye must call me Quinn, please. I would deem it the greatest honor."

Taking her soft hand in his, he cupped it reverently. How he wanted to hear his name on her lips. He didn't know what had come over him and, in truth, he didn't give a ragman's scorn. Something had clicked the instant he laid eyes upon her, and he knew as well as he knew his name that his life had inexplicably veered down a heretofore unexplored path.

It was terrifying. And exhilarating. And marvelous.

His request for her to address him by his given name lay completely outside the bounds of propriety, and yet she made no attempt to remove her hand from his. In fact, she cupped his palm back, her pale fingers in stark relief against his sun-browned skin. Her dainty, fine-boned hand nested inside his as if sculpted to fit there.

"And it would please me if you'd call me Skye," she said, a touch of color high on her cheekbones.

A secret thrill tunneled through him. She was bold in the sweetest way possible.

Eyes guileless and the merest bit curious, she curved her mouth upward. "Quinn, I know this may sound strange, and please believe me when I tell you I am not usually so forward, but I feel as if I've known you my entire life. That we aren't strangers meeting for the first time at all."

Yes, he knew exactly what she felt, because the same sensation sluiced through him.

She gave a self-conscious chuckle, and her lush lashes fanned against her porcelain skin for the space of a blink before she met his gaze again. A hint of becoming color tinged her sloping cheeks. "'Tis silly, I know."

"Nae, no' silly, Skye." He stepped nearer, drawing her close and then tipped her chin upward with one finger. "I ken exactly what ye mean, for though I canna explain it, I feel precisely the same way."

"You do?" she whispered, her breath sweet and smelling of strawberries.

"Aye, lass," he murmured before brushing his lips across

the velvety softness of her fingers. "I feel like I've come home at last."

I hope you enjoyed this free preview of
A CHRISTMAS KISS FOR THE HIGHLANDER
Heart of a Scot
Book Nine

Thank you for reading TO BARGAIN WITH A HIGHLAND BUCCANEER, the eighth in my HEART OF A SCOT series.

I know it's unusual to have a Highlander who spends more time on the ocean than in the Highlands, but Bryston's character demanded it.

I took a wee bit of author license with a few facts in this story. For instance, the great age of piracy on Tortuga ended in the late 1600s, but I extended it into the early 1700s for the purpose of this tale. Privateers received a letter of marque that basically made being a pirate legal—all for a good cause, of course. Some pirates did retire and go on to live respectable lives.

Nearly eight hundred women did volunteer to become the wives of French colonists in places like Tortuga between 1663 and 1673. They were called *Filles du Roi,* which means King's Daughters. Leith did have a street named Abbey Street, but the wharves weren't clearly visible from there. There was also a brothel called Lucky Spence's House and a tavern named the Queen's Arms.

I hope you found a few hours of relaxation and escape with Bryston and Branwen. If so, please consider leaving a review. I'd appreciate it very much! Be sure to check out the other books in my HEART OF A SCOT series too.

To make sure you don't miss any of my book news, subscribe to my newsletter (Get a free book too!). I also have a fabulous VIP Reader Group on Facebook, Collette's Chéris. If you're a fan of my books and historical romance, I'd love to have you join me. You'll also be the first to see new covers, read exclusive excerpts, be the first to know about contests and give-aways, help me pick titles and name characters, and much, much more.

Please consider telling other readers why you enjoyed this book by reviewing it as well. I also truly adore hearing from my readers. You can contact me on my www.collettecameron-books.com and while you are there, explore my author world.

Hugs,
Collette

If you haven't joined Collette's exclusive mailing list click on QR image to sign up! You'll get access to exclusive content, sneak peeks, contests, giveaways, and more...
(P.S. No spam!)

https://collettecameronbooks.com/freegift

Collette loves to hear from readers.
You can contact her via her website: collettecameron-books.com.
Or email her directly at collette@collettecameron-books.com.

You can also follow Collette on social media:
Facebook: https://www.-facebook.com/ColletteCameronNovels/
Instagram: https://instagram.com/collettecameronauthor/
Goodreads: https://www.goodreads.com/collettecameron
Book Bub: https://www.bookbub.com/authors/collette-cameron

Pinterest: http://www.pinterest.com/colletteauthor/
YouTube: https://www.youtube.com/@ColletteCamero-
nAuthor

COLLETTE CAMERON®

USA Today Bestselling author Collette Cameron® is renowned for her captivating, humorous, and heartwarming Scottish and Regency historical romance novels. With over 65 published titles, over 1.6 million books sold around the world, and multiple writing awards to her credit, Collette is a well-known author in the world of historical romance.

Readers love her witty and relatable characters including daring rogues, dashing scoundrels, and the strong and spirited heroines who capture their hearts. From the rugged highlands to the refined drawing rooms of Regency England, Collette's novels will transport you to another time and place, where love and adventure are just a page away.

Collette's Sweet-to-Spicy Timeless Romances® are the perfect escape for readers looking for romantic escape, poignant inspiration, engaging humor, and entertaining stories.

Based in the Pacific Northwest, Collette is surrounded by the lush greenery and rainy skies that inspire her writing. She dreams of one day splitting her time between the Pacific Northwest and Scotland. In the meantime, she indulges in her love of all things cobalt blue, dachshunds, chocolate, and of course, crafting her next historical romance.

Blue Rose Romance® LLC
collette@collettecameronbooks.com
collettecameronbooks.com

~

FOR THE LOVE OF AN EARL (Wicked Earls' Club)

A Humorous Aristocrat and Wallflower

Regency Romance Adventure

~

HEART OF A SCOT

A Passionate Enemies to Lovers

Scottish Highlander Historical Mystery

Romance Adventure

HIGHLAND HEATHER ROMANCING A SCOT: CASTLE BRIDES

A Passionate Enemies to Lovers Second Chance

Scottish Highlander Mystery Romance

~

LADIES OF OPPORTUNITY
**A Bluestockings and Rogues Opposites Attract
Regency Mystery Christmas Romance**

The Wallflower's Wild Wager — Book 1

The Spinster's Secret Stake, Book 2

Better Not Bet a Bluestocking – Book 3

~

SECRETS OF SCANDALOUS LADIES
**A Romantic Class Difference Forced Proximity
Regency Romance with Aristocrats**

A Lady's Scandalous Kiss — Book 1

No Lady for the Lord — Book 2

Love Lessons for a Lady — Book 3

His One and Only Lady — Book 4

Never a Proper Lady — Book 5

Lady Tempts a Rogue — Book 6

~

THE CULPEPPER MISSES
**A Humorous Wallflower Family Saga
Regency Romantic Comedy**

The Earl and the Spinster — Book 1

The Marquis and the Vixen — Book 2

The Lord and the Wallflower — Book 3

The Buccaneer and the Bluestocking — Book 4

The Lieutenant and the Lady — Book 5

~

THE HONORABLE ROGUES®
A Second Chance Redeemable Rogue
and Wallflower Regency Romance

A Kiss for a Rogue — Book 1

A Bride for a Rogue — Book 2

A Rogue's Scandalous Wish — Book 3

To Capture a Rogue's Heart — Book 4

The Rogue and the Wallflower — Book 5

A Rose for a Rogue — Book 6

'Twas the Rogue Before Christmas — Book 7

A Rogue Worth the Risk — Book 8

www.ingramcontent.com/pod-product-compliance
Lightning Source LLC
Chambersburg PA
CBHW072134300726

48975CB00003B/1064